Bullet for a Ranger

A Texas Ranger Jim Blawcyzk Story

BY JAMES J. GRIFFIN

Texas Ranger Jim Blawcyzk had awakened to find himself in the last place he'd ever expect to be: stone drunk, in a saloon woman's bed. Even worse for the lawman, the woman was alongside him, dead, with Jim's Bowie knife stuck in her chest.

Now Jim was in a cell, with the entire town of Quitaque clamoring for a quick trial and hanging. Jim's sole unlikely ally was the priest from the Catholic mission, and even the good padre had some doubts about the Ranger's innocence.

Someone in Quitaque was determined to see Jim Blawcyzk hanged for murder. If Jim didn't figure out who it was right quick, he'd soon be the guest of honor at a hemp necktie party.

* * *

Jim walked slowly toward the cell door. Castle stood aside to let him pass, his gun now aimed at the Ranger's stomach, the hammer thumbed back. When Jim drew abreast of the marshal he lunged at Castle, grabbing for his gun.

Bullet for a Ranger

A Texas Ranger Jim Blawcyzk Story
by James J. Griffin

Design and Layout by Laura Ashton
www.gitflorida.com

Copyright © 2010 by James J. Griffin
All rights reserved.

No part of this book may be used or reproduced by any means, graphic, electronic, or mechanical, including photocopying, recording, taping or by any information storage retrieval system without the express written consent of the publisher, except in the case of brief quotations embodied in critical articles and reviews.

This is a work of fiction. All of the characters, names, incidents, organizations, places, and dialogue in this novel are either the products of the author's imagination or are used fictitiously. Any resemblance to actual persons, living or dead, is strictly coincidence.

ISBN: 978-1-4528-0594-8

Printed in the United States of America

Other Texas Ranger Novels

By

James J. Griffin

Trouble Rides the Texas Pacific

Border Raiders

Trail of the Renegade

Ranger Justice

Panhandle Raiders

Big Bend Death Trap

Ranger's Revenge

The Faith and the Rangers

Death Stalks the Rangers

Coming in Fall 2010
from Condor Publishing Inc.

Ride for Redemption

For Gina, Dick, and Pete

As always, thanks to Texas Ranger Sergeant Jim Huggins of Company A, Houston, and Karl Rehn and Penny Riggs of KR Training, Manheim, Texas.

Bullet for a Ranger

A Texas Ranger Jim Blawcyzk Story

By JAMES J. GRIFFIN

Chapter One

JIM BLAWCYZK, Texas Ranger lieutenant, groggily awakened in an unfamiliar room. His head was pounding, stomach churning, and mouth dry as flannel. Sweat beaded on his forehead and plastered his blonde hair to his scalp. He started to push himself up, but fell back when the room spun like a Texas tornado. Jim felt as if he'd been thrown and stomped by a crazed bronc. He lay there, eyes closed, waiting for the vertigo to subside.

When the Ranger's senses began to return, he realized he was lying naked on top of the damp sheets. He reeked of liquor and an empty whiskey bottle, half its contents spilled over the bedcovers, was next to him. Dully, Jim ran a hand over his belly. It came away sticky with partially dried blood. Shocked fully awake, Jim jerked upright. His clear blue eyes widened with horror.

Lying alongside him was one of the women from the Quicksilver Saloon. She also was naked and covered with blood. Jim's Bowie knife was driven deep into her chest. The knife's heavy blade had pierced her heart, probably killing her almost instantly. Jim stared at the body in disbelief.

"Don't move, Ranger," a voice warned. Jim managed to look away from the dead saloon woman to see Quitaque's town marshal, Walt Castle, in a chair on the opposite side of the room. He held a sixgun leveled at Jim's chest. With the marshal were Duke Ballantine, the owner of the Quicksilver, and several of Ballantine's men.

"I reckon you're gonna swing for what you did to Jenny," Castle concluded.

Jim shook his head, attempting to clear the cobwebs from his brain. He had no recollection of the previous night, and no idea how he'd landed in that bed, let alone in the company of a woman, who now lay dead in the same bed.

"I didn't kill her," Jim objected. "In fact, I've only seen her once before, from across the barroom. I've never even talked to her. There's gotta be some explanation."

"There sure is," the marshal retorted. "You got liquored up, came upstairs with Jenny, got into an argument with her, and killed her in a drunken rage." He nodded toward the Quicksilver's owner. "Mister Ballantine here heard the noise, but by the time he got upstairs, it was too late. Jenny was dead, and you were passed out cold. Now get your pants on. Don't worry about the rest of your duds. You're headed for a cell, then a hang rope, so you won't be needin' 'em anyway. Don't bother lookin' for your gun. I've got it right here."

Castle held up Jim's gunbelt and Colt Peacemaker.

"But I didn't kill her," Jim repeated.

"You can tell that to the jury, before they hang you," Ballantine smirked.

"Get movin', Ranger, before I drill you right now," the marshal ordered. He waggled the barrel of his gun for emphasis.

Dazedly, Jim swung his legs over the side of the mattress. He found his jeans on the floor alongside the bed, picked them up and pulled them on. He stood up, swaying for a moment until he regained his equilibrium. The marshal jabbed his pistol into Jim's spine.

"Head downstairs and across to the jail," he ordered.

Jim stumbled out of the room and down the stairs, into the Quicksilver's main room. His head still splitting and stomach queasy, he barely saw the occupants of the bar, nor heard their angry calls for his lynching.

"Take it easy, boys," Ballantine ordered. "We'll give the Ranger a fair trial, then we'll hang him. Just go back to your drinks."

The threats subsided to an angry murmur.

"Keep movin', Ranger, unless you want to die right now," Castle warned. He shoved Jim through the batwings.

A moment later, Jim, Ballantine, and the marshal were at the lockup. Jim was pushed into a cell, the door slammed shut behind him.

"I hope you enjoy your new home," Castle said. "Not

that you'll be here for long. I'd imagine you'll be hung before the week is out. Ain't that right, Mister Ballantine?"

"I'd say so," the Quicksilver's owner agreed. "It's a shame to see a good lawman go bad, but I guess it happens occasionally. You should've kept your temper in check, Lieutenant. I honestly don't know if Marshal Castle here and I will be able to stop a lynching, if the town makes up its mind to that. Jenny was a mighty popular gal."

Jim started to reply, then kept silent, realizing he'd only be wasting his breath. Obviously, nothing he could say would convince the marshal or Ballantine he hadn't killed that woman. Instead, he turned away and dropped face-down on the bunk.

"Keep a close eye on him, Marshal," Ballantine ordered. "I'll be back to check on him in the morning."

"I sure will," Castle answered.

Ballantine and his men left the marshal's office. Leaving the door which separated the cells from the office open, Castle pulled off his gunbelt and boots, then stretched out on his own cot.

Jim's mind raced for a short time as he attempted to piece together the night's events. Then his fogged brain gave up the struggle, and he fell back into unconsciousness.

Chapter Two

JIM AWOKE the next morning with his head still throbbing. He hadn't touched a drop of liquor in years, ever since the day when, as a young cowboy, he and some of his partners had gotten rip-roaring drunk at the end of a long trail drive. Those hours of drinking had led to a brawl in a gambling parlor, then gunplay. Three gamblers and two of Jim's friends died that night. The next day Jim woke up in a jail cell, with no recollection of the previous night and a hangover the size of the Lone Star State. Fortunately for him, the chief houseman at the gambling parlor testified that Jim had passed out and was sprawled on the floor, out cold, at the time of the gunfight. Thanks to the man's honesty Jim had been released, with orders never to return to that cattle town. Now, once again locked in a cell and with a massive hangover, Jim's bitter memories returned.

Hearing his prisoner stir, Marshal Castle walked over to the cell. He stood gazing balefully through the bars.

"I reckon you regret killin' that woman right about now, huh, Ranger?" he sneered, blowing smoke from his cigarette in Jim's direction.

"You know I didn't kill her, Marshal," Jim snapped. "This whole thing is a frame-up. Someone wants to make sure I don't finish my business in Quitaque."

"You can deny it all you want," Castle replied, "but there were plenty of witnesses in the Quicksilver who saw you drinkin' real heavy, then go upstairs with Jenny. In addition, Duke Ballantine heard the two of you arguin', then Jenny's scream. We've got you dead to rights, Ranger."

Jim propped himself on one elbow.

"I haven't had a drink in years, not even beer," he answered. "As far as goin' upstairs with a woman, I'm a married man, and I'd never cheat on my wife. Whoever's tryin' to frame me didn't know either of those facts, or he never would've tried somethin' so clumsy. And Marshal, I'll wipe that smirk off your face once I get outta this cell and get to the bottom of this," Jim promised. "You can bet a hat on it."

"I wouldn't count on that," Castle answered. "You'll be dead and buried before the week is out. Now, it's time for me to get some breakfast. I'll bring something back for you. Never let it be said that Marshal Walt Castle abused a prisoner. I'll be a while though, since I like a leisurely meal. Don't go anywhere until I get back."

Castle laughed wickedly.

Once the door slammed behind Castle, Jim lay on his back, staring at the ceiling. Despite what he had told the marshal, Jim was certain he knew who was behind the attempt to frame him. That person had gone to a lot of trouble to make a convincing case against the Ranger.

"I'm positive Duke Ballantine put this whole scheme together," he muttered, "although I have to consider the possibility it could be someone else. That's not likely, though. However, whoever wants me dead is doin' a mighty good job of makin' sure that's gonna happen," he muttered. "I've gotta admit, this is a nice, tidy frame-up, and if I can't figure some way out of it real quick, I'll be wearin' a hemp necktie before long. And I can bet my own hat on that."

He began reviewing the events of the past few days in his mind.

Map of Texas 1886

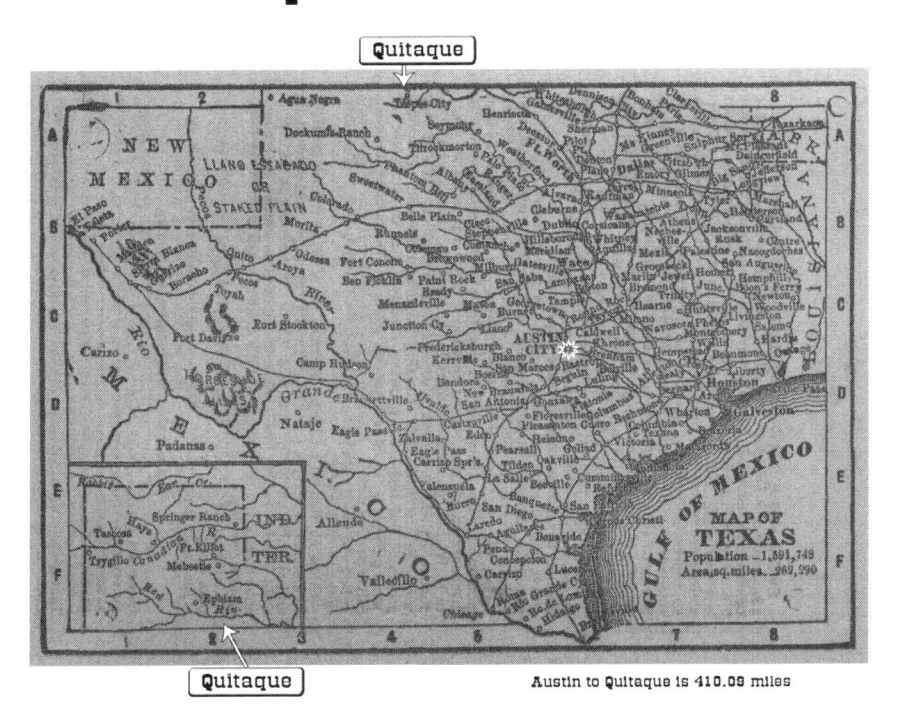

Austin to Quitaque is 410.09 miles

The name of the town to which Ranger Jim Blawcyzk was sent from Austin is Quitaque, pronounced Kit-ta-kway *or* Kitty-quay. *It is located a short distance south of the Prairie Dog Town Fork of the Red River, about 90 miles southeast of the present-day city of Amarillo. The first settlement of the area was in 1865 when a trading post was established by Jose Piedad Tayfoya, a Comanchero trader. In 1877 George Baker headquartered a herd of 2,000 cattle at the* Lazy F Ranch. *Charles Goodnight bought the Lazy F in 1880. It was Goodnight who introduced the name "Quitaque".*

There are three versions for the origin of the town's name. The first is that Goodnight believed Quitaque was an Indian word meaning "end of the trail". The second version is the name was derived from two buttes in the area which resembled horse manure, the real meaning of the Indian word. Finally, the third version claims that the name was taken from the Quitaca Indians, whose name was translated by white settlers as "Whatever one steals".

Today there are over 400 citizens living in Quitaque, Texas.

Chapter Three

Jim had been ordered to Quitaque in response to a complaint from John Baker, a distant cousin of George Baker. Until 1877, when George Baker had driven a herd of two thousand head of cattle to the area and founded the Lazy F Ranch, Quitaque hadn't even been a dot on the Texas map. Its only claim to fame was as the former site of a trading post operated by Comanchero trader Jose Piedad Tayfoya. Tayfoya had opened the post in 1865, but abandoned it in 1867, a mere two years later. For the next ten years, until Baker and his herd arrived, the site had been mostly ignored. Baker's Lazy F prospered, so much so that in 1880 he was able to sell the ranch to the famed Charles Goodnight. It was Goodnight who had named the settlement Quitaque.

While the town was located on the vast plains of the Texas Panhandle, it was also close by the Caprock, the rocky escarpment which divides the Llano Estacado and High Plains from the lower lands to the south and east. The eroded cliffs, canyons and breaks of the Caprock afforded plenty of hiding places for rustlers and outlaws, along with the occasional band of Indians raiding from the Territories. Ranchers attracted by the rich grass of the plains had to contend with the theft of their livestock on an almost daily basis. Cattle rustling, however, was not what had been on Captain Hank Trumbull's mind when he summoned Jim to his office.

"Good mornin', Jim. You want some coffee?" Trumbull greeted his Lieutenant, when Jim stepped through his office door. "I've also brought some fresh muffins from home for you. Maisie made them special. I've even kept them warm on the stove."

"Uh-oh. I must really be in for it this time," Jim replied, with a grin. "You never bring me treats from your wife unless you've got somethin' up your sleeve, Cap'n... like a job no one else will take."

"That's the problem with you, Lieutenant. Your suspicious nature. I'm surprised you think these nice, warm muffins are a bribe," Trumbull answered.

"I don't think they are. I know," Jim retorted. "But that doesn't mean I won't take 'em, and that coffee too. You know my price, Cap'n."

"Yup. Food," Trumbull laughed. "Take a seat while I fetch your breakfast."

While Jim settled on a battered leather couch, Trumbull filled a mug with thick, black coffee, placed several muffins on a plate, and handed them to the lieutenant. He then poured himself a cup of coffee, sat behind his scarred oak desk, and took out a beat-up pipe from his vest pocket. He filled the pipe, lit it, and took several puffs. After blowing a ring of smoke toward the ceiling, he opened the file on his desk.

"How's that muffin, Jim?" he asked.

"Real delicious, Cap'n," Jim answered, through a mouthful of pastry. "If I were home more often, between Julia's and your wife's cookin', before long I'd be too fat to climb into the saddle."

"That'd take some doin'," Trumbull responded, eyeing the lanky Blawcyzk. Jim was a shade over six feet tall, with broad shoulders and chest, but lean through the hips, and flat-bellied. "Besides, you don't have to worry about hangin' around here, gettin' fat and lazy. It's been a while since you've been up in the Panhandle, hasn't it?"

"It has been quite a spell, yeah," Jim confirmed.

"Then it's high time you took another run up that way," Trumbull answered. "To Quitaque, to be precise."

"Quitaque? That ain't much of a place," Jim answered. "How much trouble could there be in Quitaque that you're bribing me with your wife's baking to head clear up there?"

"There's more than enough to keep you occupied," Trumbull explained. "The usual cattle rustlin' and horse stealin', of course. Quitaque's close enough to the Caprock that there's lots of places to hide stolen stock. Plenty of other renegades use the Caprock to disappear, too. That's a year's work for a Ranger right there, rounding up the outlaws who use those canyons for their hideouts. Then there's the occasional raids by Comanches and Kiowas who sneak off their reservations in the Territories. Don't forget, it's not even that far a run to the Palo Duro from the area. But none of that's your concern, except if you happen to run across a man on our Fugitive List, or an Indian raiding party."

"Then why're you sendin' me up there?"

Trumbull shuffled through the file on his desk. His frosty blue eyes fixed Jim with a steady gaze.

"This here's a complaint from John Baker. He's some kind of kin to George Baker."

"George Baker? You mean the hombre who started the Lazy F Ranch, then sold it to Charlie Goodnight?"

"The same," Trumbull confirmed. "Although John's not a rancher, or so it seems. He's a businessman in Quitaque. His letter says he's got a general store, hotel, and runs the feed store. He also owns a saloon, the Panhandle Palace. In addition, he's on the town council. From what I've been able to determine, Baker seems to be a square shooter."

"But there's a problem."

"There sure is, if what Baker writes is true. He claims there's a bad element tryin' to take over the town. A couple new saloons and gamblin' halls have opened up, not to mention a sporting house or two."

"There's nothing unusual about saloons and gamblin' places in a cow town, Cap'n," Jim dryly noted.

"I know that, Lieutenant," Trumbull shot back. "Just

keep shut and listen. Accordin' to Baker, the new element's tryin' to push the established businesses out of their way. There's been threats and vandalism, broken windows, smashed buckboards, things like that. Some of the store owners have been roughed up. Apparently it's gettin' worse, from what Baker writes. In the past few weeks, there've been some shootin's, and at least three men have been killed. Baker says the town marshal hasn't been able to do anything."

"You don't think mebbe this is just a fight between rival factions for control of the liquor, gambling, and women in Quitaque?" Jim asked.

"I don't believe so," Trumbull answered. "Baker's well-respected up there. He's got a wife and three daughters, so it seems to me he'd have too much to lose by gettin' tangled up in something like that. I have a gut feelin' his complaints are legitimate."

"Well, your gut instincts have always been good enough for me, Cap'n," Jim said. "However, what about Charlie Goodnight? I'm kinda surprised he's not takin' a hand in this, since he still owns the *Lazy F*."

"Goodnight's already got his plate full, what with his ranch in the Palo Duro takin' up most of his time. I'd imagine he's just gonna let this situation play out, unless things get too far outta hand. That's gonna be your job, Jim, to make sure they don't."

"I understand, Cap'n. Did Baker give you any idea who he thinks is behind all the trouble?"

"Yeah, he did. The person he mentions is an hombre

name of Duke Ballantine. You ever hear of him?"

"I can't say as I have."

"I don't recollect the name either and I haven't been able to find out anything about him. Baker claims Ballantine came into town a few months ago. He opened a place called the Quicksilver. According to Baker, Ballantine brought a rough bunch along. He also claims the trouble started shortly after Ballantine arrived."

"Sounds like I'll need to check into this Ballantine fella right off," Jim noted.

"That's where I'd start," Trumbull agreed. "How soon can you leave?"

"Sizzle, Sam, and I are ready to head out right now," Jim answered. "It's about a two week ride up to the Panhandle, but if I push hard we can make it in ten days or so."

"I'd appreciate it if you'd do just that," Trumbull replied. "It looks like Quitaque might be settin' on a powder keg. I want you to get up there before somethin' or someone lights the fuse which sets it off."

Jim stood up. He took the remaining muffins from the plate on Trumbull's stove.

"I'll be ridin'. Tell Maisie thanks for the muffins. I'll just tuck these last few in my saddlebags."

"You're welcome to them. You be careful, Jim," Trumbull warned.

"I always am, Cap'n," Jim assured him. "*Adios.*"

Trumbull looked out his window to watch Jim head for the hitchrail where the lieutenant's big paint geldings, Sizzle and Sam, waited. Sizzle wore Jim's saddle and the rest of his gear, while Sam carried a light pack rig. Sam had been Jim's Ranger trail horse for years, until he was badly injured during an attack on Jim's home and family. Now, still always ready to hit the trail, but unable to carry the Ranger's weight, Sam carried Jim's extra supplies. The horses nuzzled their rider's hip pocket, begging for one of the ever-present peppermints Jim kept there for them. After giving each mount a candy, Jim untied Sam's lead line and tucked it into a saddlebag. The horse would stick with the Ranger without being led. Jim then tightened his cinches, untied Sizzle's reins, and tossed them over the paint's neck. He swung into the saddle. Jim backed Sizzle away from the rail, Sam alongside, then headed up Capitol Avenue.

"Those two cayuses are as opposite as can be," Trumbull chuckled while he watched Jim ride out. "Sizzle's as friendly a bronc as I've seen, while Sam's the most ornery critter I've ever come across. They're kinda like Jim himself that way. Jim's the easiest-goin', friendliest cuss you'd ever want to meet, unless you're a lawbreaker. Then he turns into a wildcat. Hombres who make the mistake of tanglin' with him generally live to regret it… if they live at all."

Trumbull's gaze followed the lieutenant until he loped out of sight.

* * *

It was early afternoon ten days later when Jim reached Quitaque. He reined in for a moment at the edge of town. At first glance, he liked what he saw of the place. Unlike so many new frontier settlements, with their hastily thrown-together, false-fronted buildings of raw lumber, usually unpainted, the structures along Quitaque's main street were considerably more substantial. Most of them appeared well-constructed, one or two even made of brick. Almost all sported a fresh coat of paint, and the signs hanging in front of the business establishments hadn't yet succumbed to the harsh Texas sun. Their lettering was still vividly colored.

"This is a nice-lookin' town. You'll get stalls, rubdowns, and a good feedin' shortly," Jim promised his paints. "I'm lookin' forward to puttin' on the feedbag, takin' a nice hot bath, and findin' a comfortable bed myself. Reckon I'll scout around a bit tonight, then hit the sack early. I'll look up John Baker in the morning. C'mon. Let's go find the livery stable."

Jim put Sizzle into a slow jog, while Sam trotted alongside. A few people glanced up as they headed down the middle of the dusty street, but most paid them no attention at all. There was nothing about Jim to attract much interest, other than the usual curiosity at any new arrival in town. Jim wanted his status as a lawman to remain unknown for the time being, so his Texas Ranger badge was snugged inside his shirt pocket. After ten days on the trail, he sported a thick growth of blonde whiskers stubbling his jaw, and his hair brushed his collar. His clothes were coated with dust and sweat stained. Sizzle and Sam were also dust-covered, and had been thinned down considerably by the hard run from Austin to the Panhandle. Their usually shiny coats were dull, their manes and tails matted with dirt and burrs. Jim looked like any one of the thousands of drifters passing through the Southwest.

Jim sat slumped casually in the saddle, but his blue eyes missed little while he rode through town and studied the people on the street and the buildings he passed. John Baker's feed and general stores occupied the same block. Across an alley from them was a three story structure, with balconies surrounding all three floors on three sides of the building. A sign running the length of the front declared this to be "Baker's Panhandle Plaza Hotel", in bright red letters.

"Baker seems to be doin' pretty well for himself," Jim murmured. "It should be a real interesting conversation with him. Wonder where his saloon is located?" He rode another two blocks, until he spotted an arrow-shaped sign pointing down a wide alleyway. "Brennan's Horse Heaven Livery Stable. Horses Sold, Traded, and Boarded. The Finest in Equine Care." it read.

"Horse Heaven? Huh. As if you two aren't already spoiled enough," Jim said, with a pat to Sizzle's neck. Sam gave a snort. "Well, let's check it out, and get you settled in." He turned into the alley, and rode to the large whitewashed barn at the end. The doors at each end of the stable were opened to catch any possible breeze. A middle-aged man, who had a neatly-trimmed gray beard framing his jaw, watched the Ranger's approach. Incongruously, the hostler was wearing a black top hat. Even more incredibly, his hat, as well his clothes, showed not a speck of dust or dirt.

"Good afternoon, sir," he greeted Jim, in an unmistakably British accent. A broad smile crossed his face. "I am Chauncey Brennan, the Third. Late of Liverpool, and for the past several months a resident of this fair town of Quitaque, Texas. Might I assume you are searching for stalls and respite for your horses?"

"You might indeed," Jim answered, as he reined up and dismounted. "I'm Jim. This is Sizzle and Sam. We've been traveling for quite a spell. They'll both need a good grainin', water, and plenty of hay."

"What about grooming? Perhaps even bathing? You have two fine-looking animals under all that dirt."

"For my horses, or myself?" Jim quipped.

"I must say, you could use a trim and washing. I can toss you in the horse trough if you'd like," Brennan retorted, with a laugh. He didn't press Jim for a last name. One thing the Englishman had learned quickly upon his arrival in Texas was not to ask too many questions.

"I wouldn't doubt that for a minute," Jim answered, grinning, for despite Brennan's dudish manners, the liveryman was broad-shouldered and well-muscled under his light gray cotton shirt. He would be a man to contend with in a fistfight. "But I reckon just for my horses. I'll handle that myself, if you don't mind. Sizzle here's a right friendly cuss, but Sam'll take a chunk out of your hide if you get too close. He's a one-man animal."

Sizzle was already nuzzling Brennan's chest. The sorrel overo had taken an instant liking to him. Sam, however, was standing close alongside Jim. The palomino and white splotched tobiano had his ears pinned at the hostler.

"I'll wager Samuel will take to me," Brennan disagreed. "Let's find out." He patted Sizzle's nose, then stepped over to Sam. He placed a gentle hand on the gelding's shoulder. When Sam twisted his head to snap at Brennan's arm, the liveryman stepped aside just enough so Sam missed. As he did, he held out his hand. Sam stopped short, ears pricked forward, and snatched the peppermint Brennan had hidden in his palm.

"Now Samuel, that's not very good etiquette, biting the hand that's going to feed you," Brennan chided. He again placed his hand on Sam's shoulder. Sam tensed, pinned his ears, and bared his teeth. "Easy, boy," Brennan soothed, "Trust me, and we'll get along just fine." He slowly massaged Sam's shoulder, gradually working his way up his neck, then rubbed his muzzle. Little by little, Sam's muscles unwound. Finally, with a loud sigh, the horse relaxed and gave a huge yawn. Brennan rewarded him with another peppermint. Sizzle nuzzled Brennan's shoulder, and was also rewarded with a candy.

"I told you Samuel would behave for me," Brennan grinned. "Now will you turn him over to me for full care?"

"Samuel? His name's Sam, unless you mean Sam-mule, as in stubborn as a Missouri jackass. You've gotta be pretty special for Sam to let you handle him," Jim said. "How'd you know he likes peppermints? I always keep some in my back pocket for him and Siz."

"You horse has the dignity of a Samuel, not a Sam. And most horses appreciate peppermints, as well as gentle handling," Brennan explained. "Too many men make the error of trying to break a horse, rather than gentling it. Breaking a horse will give you a mount you can ride, certainly, but there can never be a true bond between human and equine when a horse's spirit is broken, sir."

"Chauncey, you and I are goin' to get along just fine, as long as you stop callin' me 'sir'," Jim chuckled. "The name's Jim. Tell you what. We can both work on these broncs. It's gonna take a while to clean them up proper."

"Splendid!" Brennan answered. "Bring them inside, and put them in the two stalls halfway-down on the left. The tack room is opposite that. You may store your equipment there. I'll remove Samuel's pack for you."

Jim led his horses into a spotlessly clean barn. The center aisle was wide, free of scattered straw or manure. The stalls into which he placed Sam and Sizzle were spacious and airy. Tools were neatly stored on a rack inside the tack room.

"You're not exaggerating when you call this place Horse Heaven, Chauncey," Jim praised, as he lifted the saddle from Sizzle's back.

"Thank you, Jim," Brennan answered. "I feel horses are the Creator's most noble beasts, and their company is preferable to that of most men, as far as I am concerned. They deserve treatment at least as good."

"I won't argue with you there," Jim agreed. "Sizzle and Sam here are pretty much my best friends. They're certainly my partners."

"I know that. I can pretty much tell whether a man respects his horse the first moment I meet him," Brennan said.

While Jim went to work on Sam's sweat-encrusted hide, Brennan filled both horse's mangers with grain, topped off their water buckets, and forked hay into their stalls. Once that was done, he took a currycomb to Sizzle. Jim and Brennan worked for over an hour, combing the dirt, dried sweat, and burrs out of the horses' coats. They then took both mounts outside, soaking them thoroughly and sponging them off.

When they were finished, Jim wiped sweat from his brow.

"They sure look a lot better'n we arrived. Thanks, Chauncey."

"That's what you're paying me for," Brennan answered. "And speaking of payment, the charge is seventy-five cents per night, each horse. Grooming was a dollar. Since we worked together, I'll only charge you for grooming one animal."

"That's fair enough," Jim agreed. He dug in his pocket, and removed a gold double eagle and two silver dollars. "I'm not sure how long I'll be in town, so here's two weeks in advance, plus the grooming charge."

"That's fine. Thank you. Let's get these two back inside before they decide to break loose and roll, which would undo all our hard work," Brennan advised.

The horses were placed back in their stalls, where both fell to munching on their remaining hay. Jim slapped each fondly on the neck, and gave them both a peppermint. Sizzle nuzzled his shoulder, while Sam, as always, buried his muzzle in Jim's belly.

"I'll check on both of you in the morning," Jim assured them, "Now behave yourselves." He lifted his saddlebags from where he'd left them on the wall of Sizzle's stall and draped them over his shoulder.

"They'll be just fine," Brennan assured him. "I have two rooms over the stable, so I'm here all night. No one will disturb your horses. I sleep with a double-barreled shotgun to make sure of that."

"Speaking of sleeping and currying, I could sure use both," Jim laughed. "Not to mention a drink or two. I'm parched. Is there anyplace you'd recommend?"

"Certainly," Brennan answered. "There are a couple of hotels here, but the Panhandle Plaza is the only decent choice. They also have a fine restaurant. Right across the street from the Plaza is Charlie's Barber Shop. He'll fix you up with a bath and shave."

"What about those drinks? I didn't spot any saloons on my way in."

"There are several pubs, or saloons as you Texans call them, here in Quitaque. They're all on the west end of town, so you must have come in from the east. Any of them are good, but I'd recommend either the Panhandle Palace or the Quicksilver. The Palace is owned by the same person as the Plaza hotel, John Baker."

"I reckon I'll check into the hotel first, clean up a bit, then try the Palace," Jim decided. "I can stand one more night without that bath. I'll take care of it in the morning."

"That offer to dump you in the horse trough still stands," Brennan laughed.

"I think I'll pass on your most kind and generous offer," Jim replied. "I'll be by in the morning. Hasta la vista, Chauncey."

"Good afternoon to you, Jim."

Jim walked up the alley to the main street, then turned toward the Panhandle Plaza, where the sounds of a scuffle caught his attention. A small crowd had gathered in front of Baker's Mercantile, two blocks ahead. They were surrounding several men, who were accosting a farmer and his family. Curses and threats rose on the still air.

"Reckon I'd better see what that's all about," Jim muttered. He loosened his Colt in its holster, then broke into a run. Just as he reached the scene, the farmer was pulled from his buckboard and dumped on the ground. Two of his attackers commenced viciously kicking him in the ribs, while the others tossed supplies from the buckboard. Helplessly, his wife and three children huddled in fear on the wagon seat.

"You were warned what would happen if you kept buyin' your goods at Baker's place, Hennessey," one of the men snarled. He kicked the farmer in the ribs again, then grabbed his shirtfront and pulled him to his feet. He sank a punch into the farmer's gut and drove another to his face. The farmer collapsed, rolled onto hands and knees, then covered his head with his arms in an attempt to ward off further blows.

Jim pulled out his sixgun and elbowed his way through the spectators, just as the gang's leader drew back his foot for another kick to the farmer's belly. Jim fired, knocking the heel from the man's boot and sending him sprawling on his back.

"The next one'll be right through your guts. Bet a hat on it," Jim warned. "Now you'd better explain what this is all about, and right quick."

"This ain't none of your affair, stranger," one of the men on the wagon warned. "You'd better put up that gun and get outta here, before you get hurt."

"I'm makin' it my business," Jim answered. "I get kinda riled when I see five hombres gangin' up on one, especially when his wife and kids are watchin'."

"Mebbe he'd like to try takin' on all of us, Hardy," one of the two men at the wagon's tailgate suggested to the man whose boot Jim had ruined. He still lay where he'd fallen, glaring at the Ranger.

"Yeah, mebbe he would at that," Hardy sneered. He pulled off his boots, pushed himself to his feet, and hobbled over to stand with the rest of his men.

"How about it, mister? You're pretty eager to stick your nose where it doesn't belong. Think you can take all five of us?"

"Five to one odds seem about right," Jim shrugged. He slid his Colt back in its holster and tossed his saddlebags on the ground.

"Make that five to two odds."

Bullet for a Ranger

The farmer had struggled to his feet. He now stood alongside Jim, fists clenched.

"You're both gonna be sorry," Hardy warned. He stepped forward and launched a punch at Jim's chin. The Ranger easily twisted away from the blow and sank a fist deep into Hardy's belly. Hardy folded into a knee to his chin. He crumpled to the dirt.

Three of the other men charged Jim, the last going after Hennessey. Jim slammed his nearest attacker in the ear, driving him back. The man stumbled into one of his partners, their feet tangling. They went down in a heap. The third man staggered Jim with a sharp blow to his jaw, then followed that with a left to Jim's gut. Air whooshed from the Ranger's lungs with the impact. Jim shook his head, dragged air back into his tormented lungs, and fought off the effects of the punch. When his adversary closed in for a finishing blow, Jim deflected the punch with his forearm, smashed a right to the man's ribs, then a shot to the jaw. The man stumbled against the wagon, groaned, and toppled to the dirt.

Hennessey, despite his injured ribs, had made short work of his opponent, felling him with several short, sharp blows to the face. He stood alongside Jim as the two men remaining in the fight scrambled to their feet. More wary now, they closed in on the Ranger and farmer.

One came in low at Jim, attempting to head-butt him in the stomach. Jim sidestepped and drove a fist to the back of the man's neck. The outlaw pitched to his face, sliding for a foot from his momentum, then lay unmoving.

Hennessey took two shots to the ribs from his opponent, then dispatched the man with a punch to the chest, followed by one to the throat. His tormentor dropped, gagging as he struggled for breath.

Jim and Hennessey staggered to the buckboard. They leaned against its side, chests heaving.

"Thanks, Mister," the farmer gasped. "Reckon I'm beholden to you. My name's Hennessey. Ben Hennessey."

He held out his hand. Jim took it.

"I'm Jim Blawcyzk."

They shook hands.

"What was this all about, Ben?" Jim asked.

"I guess I should explain," Hennessey began. He was interrupted by a warning from one of the bystanders.

"Marshal Castle's comin'."

A moment later, a man wearing a town marshal's star pushed his way through the crowd. He glanced at the five men still sprawled in the road, then glared at Jim. His brown eyes fixed the Ranger with an irate stare.

"What's the meaning of this?" he demanded, his face contorted with anger.

"These five hombres were gangin' up on this man. That didn't seem fair, so I took a hand," Jim shrugged.

"Two of those men are my deputies. If they were attempting to detain Hennessey they had good reason. What gives you the right to attack officers of the law? You're under arrest, cowboy."

Castle's right hand edged toward his pistol. In a blur, Jim's left hand slashed downward and pulled his heavy Peacemaker from its holster. Jim leveled the gun and pointed it just above the marshal's belt buckle. Castle froze, his hand still three inches above the butt of his six-gun. He saw instant death in Jim's eyes, which glittered like chips of blue ice.

"I'd say this Colt aimed straight at your belly pretty much gives me the right," Jim snapped. "However, just in case that's not enough to convince you, how about this?"

Jim fumbled in his shirt pocket, removed his Ranger badge, and pinned it to his vest.

"A Ranger!" someone exclaimed, at the sight of the silver star on silver circle glittering on Jim's chest. While Rangers wore no uniforms, and the majority still didn't wear badges, more and more of them were carrying those silver stars on silver circles, most hand-carved from a Mexican five or ten peso coin. The symbol conveyed instant authority.

"That's right. I'm a Texas Ranger," Jim confirmed. "Now all of you go on about your business. And Marshal, you take your deputies and their pardners and get 'em outta here… before I make a few arrests of my own."

"You win… for now, Ranger," Castle grumbled. "But this isn't the last of it. Not by a long shot."

"You might want to think twice about makin' threats like that," Jim warned. "Now git!"

"All right. C'mon, Hardy. Take your men and get outta here," Castle ordered.

Once the marshal and his men had stalked away, Hennessey said to Jim, "Walt Castle's not a man to cross, Ranger."

"I've come across men like him plenty of times," Jim responded. "You're right. He'll bear watching, but he probably won't make another move for a while. Let's get your stuff loaded back up, so you can head home. And by the way, you haven't introduced me to that pretty lady on your wagon."

"Ranger, with all the excitement, I plumb forgot!" Hennessey apologized. He turned to the buckboard. "Jim, this is my wife Louise. Lou, Ranger Jim Blah… Blah… Heck, how'd you say your last name, Ranger?"

"Bluh-zhick. It's Polish," Jim explained.

"Ranger Blawcyzk. Jim, the kids are Ben Junior, Susan, and Belle."

"Mrs. Hennessey." Jim touched two fingers to the brim of his Stetson in greeting. "Call me Jim. It's easier."

"Of course… Jim. But you must call me Louise. I'm very grateful for you helping drive off Joe Hardy and his band of bullies."

"I have to admit I enjoyed it," Jim confessed. "It appears they needed to be brought down a notch."

"I got a lot of satisfaction out of it, too," Hennessey stated. "Maybe that pack of wolves will finally think twice about pushin' folks around."

"Which brings me back to my question. Why were those hombres pickin' on you, Ben?" Jim asked.

"Because I won't knuckle under to 'em and stop tradin' with John Baker," Hennessey explained. "Someone's tryin' to drive Baker and the other honest merchants in town out of business. Anyone who doesn't cave in, and stays a customer of John's, is liable to get the same treatment you just saw. Most folks have already given in, but there's still a few of us who won't."

Hennessey tossed a sack of flour into the buckboard, then glanced up.

"Speakin' of John Baker, here he comes now."

A stocky individual, of slightly less than average height, was hurrying across the street. He was dressed in a brown business suit, his head covered by a narrow-brimmed brown Stetson. A gold watch chain was draped across his vest. He stopped once he reached Hennessey and Jim.

"Ben, my store clerk told me what happened. Are you and your family all right?"

"We are, thanks to the Ranger here," Hennessey replied.

"Yes. My clerk also told me about that. I'm John Baker, Ranger...?"

"Lieutenant Jim Blawcyzk. I'm glad I was able to help."

"Are you here in answer to my letter to Ranger Headquarters?" Baker asked.

"I am." Jim glanced down at the badge pinned to his vest. "I was plannin' on keeping my identity secret for a while, so I could do some snoopin' around quietly, but I guess that idea's shot to pieces," he chuckled.

"I'm grateful Austin responded to my request so quickly. We'll have to talk the first chance you get. Have you settled on a place to stay?"

"I was headed over to your hotel, but sorta got sidetracked," Jim smiled. "Chauncey at the livery stable recommended it."

"Chauncey Brennan the Third," Baker laughed. "Someday I'll get that hombre to tell me how he came to leave England and land in Quitaque, Texas, of all places. Nevertheless, I'm grateful to him for sending clients my way. You'll stay at the Plaza as long as you are here in town, Lieutenant. Of course, there will be no charge for the room, or your meals," Baker concluded.

"I'll be glad to stay at your place, but I can't take up your offer of free board and lodging. Even if it wasn't considered a bribe, that would give the wrong impression. It'd look like I was already takin' up your side, Mister Baker," Jim explained. "So I'll pay my own way. Even then some folks will talk."

"I understand. Rest assured, I certainly didn't mean the offer as a bribe," Baker apologized. "But I will have a room ready whenever you need it."

"I'll help Ben here finish loading his wagon, then I'll be over to the hotel," Jim answered. "As far as that talk, I just want to take tonight and get a good supper and a good night's sleep. I'll meet with you in the morning."

"That's fine with me," Baker answered. "How about

around eight o'clock, at my office in the hotel? That's not too early, is it?"

"I'm always up with the sun," Jim answered. "Eight o'clock's the middle of the morning for me."

"Good. I'll see you then. I'd better return, so I can send my clerk back to the store. He'll help you reload your wagon, Ben."

Baker headed for the hotel.

"Ben, let's get finished here, so you can be on your way. You'd better get those bruised ribs cared for as soon as you can, too," Jim told the farmer. "Mebbe I should get my horse and follow you home, just in case Hardy and his men try something again."

"There's no need for that, Jim. We gave them a pretty good thrashing. They'll probably head for the Quicksilver and lick their wounds. That's where they hang out when they're not stirrin' up trouble."

"As long as you're certain," Jim answered.

"We are," Louise spoke up. "But I do insist you come out to our farm for supper, as soon as possible. It's the least we can do for you."

"I'll be glad to," Jim replied. "As soon as I have a couple of days to do some investigating."

"That's fine. Whenever you wish, just ride out to our farm," Louise answered. "It's three and a half-miles southeast of here. There's a sign which reads Hennessey's Farm nailed to a large cottonwood, so you can't miss the place. We'll be waiting."

"My wife's the best cook in the Panhandle. It'll be worth your while, Jim," Hennessey added.

"Then I'll make sure and get there soon," Jim promised.

With the help of Matt, a teen-aged clerk from the Mercantile, Ben's wagon was quickly reloaded. Jim watched the Hennesseys drive out of town, then picked up his saddlebags and started for the hotel. Already, his plans had gone awry. Instead of him apparently being a drifting cowpoke who would attract little attention, by morning most of Quitaque would know he was a Texas Ranger. His job had just become much more difficult.

* * *

After their whipping, Joe Hardy and his men headed for the Quicksilver Saloon. Hardy's dark eyes still glittered with anger, and his brown hair was matted with blood. He kept a hand pressed to his belly, rubbing the sore spot where Jim's punch had landed.

"Tell Duke we need to talk, Tom," Hardy ordered the man behind the bar. "Leave a bottle and some glasses first."

"Sure, Joe. Whatever you say," Tom Doyle shrugged. The saloon man was well into middle-age, and merely wanted to spend the rest of his days serving drinks and avoiding trouble, not an easy task in a frontier bar. Doyle placed a bottle of whiskey and five glasses on the mahogany, then disappeared behind a door marked "Private". Hardy and the rest had barely poured their first drinks when Doyle reappeared, trailed by Duke Ballantine, the Quicksilver's owner. Ballantine looked over the battered group before speaking, his words clipped and deliberate.

"Tom said you needed to see me, Joe," he said. "Did you take care of Hennessey like you were ordered? Or, judging from your appearances, did that farmer give you a sound thumping?"

"It wasn't Hennessey who did most of this, Duke," Hardy answered. He rubbed the lump on his jaw. "There's a Texas Ranger in town. He surprised us, and he buffaloed Walt Castle, too. Got the drop on him before Castle even touched his gun. That Ranger's got the fastest draw I've ever seen. He sure wasn't any slouch with his fists, either."

"What's that? There's a Ranger here?"

"Sure is," Hardy confirmed. "Said his name was Jim Blawcyzk, or somethin' like that. Big blonde hombre. He's got blue eyes that'll bore right through you."

"I don't like the idea of the Rangers snoopin' around, Duke," Mike Putney said. Putney was a hot-tempered redhead.

"I'm not happy about it, either," Ballantine replied.

"I could bushwhack that Ranger real easy, Duke," Hardy proposed. "A bullet in the back'd take care of him for good."

"Don't be stupid," Ballantine said. "If the Ranger turns up dead there'll be a dozen more here in less than a week.

Killin' him's a real bad idea."

"Mebbe we could just lay low for a spell," Dude Bannon suggested. The stocky outlaw continued, "If that Ranger can't come up with something, after awhile he'll ride on out and go back to Austin."

"We can't chance that," Ballantine answered. "We don't have that much time, and every day the Ranger is in town the more men'll be willing to stand up against me. No, that won't work."

"Well, if we can't kill him, and we can't let him poke around, then what do we do?" Hardy asked.

"Give me a little time. I'll come up with something," Ballantine answered. "Until I do, don't pull any rough stuff. You boys are going to be model citizens."

"What if that Ranger comes to talk to you, Duke?" Bannon asked.

"I'm sure he will, and I want him to," Ballantine explained. "I'll do my best to convince him I'm an honest businessman trying to make a decent living. It will also give me the chance to size him up. Perhaps I'll find a weakness I can exploit."

"So what do we do in the meantime?" Hardy asked.

"Just stay out of trouble. Spend the rest of the day here with your liquor and cards. While you do that, I'm going to talk to Walt Castle. I need to make sure that Ranger hasn't turned up a yellow streak in our fine marshal. And don't worry, I'll take care of the Ranger," Ballantine promised. "It just has to be done carefully. See you boys later."

*   *   *

Jim had considered stopping by the Quicksilver and talking with Duke Ballantine after the Hennesseys left for home. However, wanting to get a good meal and night's sleep after his hard ride from Austin, he decided to put off any confrontation with the man until the next day.

His second-floor room at the Panhandle Plaza was spacious and clean. Surprisingly for a frontier hostelry, the bed was soft and comfortable. More tired than he'd realized, Jim slept until almost seven. He'd found out Charlie's Barber Shop wouldn't open until nine, so he cleaned up as best he could at the washstand in his room, ate a hearty breakfast in the hotel restaurant, and checked on his horses. They had both been fed, and were now stretched out on their sides in one of the livery's corrals, dozing in the early morning sun. They didn't even bother to come to the fence for a peppermint.

At eight, Jim was back at the hotel, where John Baker was waiting for him.

"Good morning, Lieutenant. I appreciate a man who's on time," Baker greeted him. "Please, have a seat. Would you like some coffee, or perhaps a cigar?"

"Just black coffee, thanks. I don't smoke," Jim answered. He settled into a brown leather chair.

"Fine." Baker poured a cupful of coffee from a pot on the sideboard and handed it to the Ranger. He then took a long cigar from a humidor on his desk and lit up.

"All right. I'm certain you have quite a few questions for me, Lieutenant. I'll answer them as best I can."

"I appreciate that. Captain Trumbull showed me your correspondence to him. You seem certain Duke Ballantine is the person responsible for most of the trouble here in Quitaque," Jim answered.

"I am," Baker confirmed. "I have no proof, of course. However, before Ballantine arrived there were no problems here to speak of, other than the usual petty thefts, and the occasional brawl in one of the saloons. Since Ballantine showed up, all Hell has broken loose, if you'll pardon the expression. Property damage, threats, attacks like the one you saw on the Hennesseys yesterday, even shootings."

"Your letter mentioned three men had been killed. The marshal hasn't done anything about all this?"

"Walt Castle? He's Ballantine's man," Baker snorted. "Since I wrote Ranger Headquarters, Stan Tuttle, our former marshal, quit, then left town. Stan wasn't a young man, and I'm convinced he was told to leave Quitaque or get a bullet in the back. He as much as admitted that before he headed for parts unknown. But again, there's no proof. Once Stan left, Ballantine recommended Castle to replace him. Given that no one else wanted the job, the town council agreed. They hired Castle, and since then things have only gotten worse. Now the troublemakers strike with impunity."

"All right, I understand what you're saying," Jim replied. "But Ballantine's businesses are his saloon and gambling halls. If he is the man behind all this trouble, why is he going after legitimate shopkeepers?"

"I'm convinced he's trying to turn Quitaque into a wide-open town. He'd like to see the main street lined with his saloons, gambling places, and brothels," Baker explained. "That would drive the most of the decent folks away. Quitaque's just startin' to get on its feet, and it's got a real future. Unfortunately, if Ballantine gets his way, he'll destroy the town."

"You still have no proof, other than the fact the trouble started after Ballantine moved here," Jim pointed out. "The Rangers have no records at all on him, so we know nothing about his background."

"He's kept things close to his vest, as you can imagine," Baker answered. "All he's told anyone who asks is that he came here from Kansas, where he was a partner in a saloon and gambling establishment. He claims he left that business to strike out on his own."

"Okay, I'll admit that Ballantine is definitely the most likely suspect, at least from what you're telling me," Jim answered. "However, I've got to consider every angle, and every possible suspect... including you, Mister Baker."

"Me? That's ridiculous," Baker snapped. "Why would I write to the Rangers for help if I were stirring up trouble?"

"Exactly," Jim answered. "What better way to take suspicion off yourself?"

"But my properties and customers have suffered the majority of the attacks," Baker protested. "You saw Hardy and his men go after Ben Hennessey for patronizing my store."

"Again, what better way to divert suspicion from

you?" Jim answered. "Maybe you hired Hardy and his bunch, then told them to hang around the Quicksilver so folks'd assume they're workin' for Baker. And maybe *you* told Marshal Tuttle to leave, or else."

"That's absurd," Baker objected.

"Not so much," Jim answered, "I'm not sayin' I put much stock in that theory, just that it is feasible. I can't discount any possibility, no matter how far-fetched."

"All right, I'll give you that. But you're wrong, Lieutenant."

"I won't dispute that, for now," Jim replied. "I will say my investigation will be thorough and impartial, no matter where it leads."

"That's all I ask," Baker answered.

"Good. Now, I'm going to visit the marshal's office. I want to look over his records. If what you say is true, I'm not sure how accurate they'll be. Could you prepare a list of incidents for me which you believe are connected?"

"I certainly will. I'll have it for you by noon."

"Fine. I'll see you then."

"Thank you, Lieutenant."

"Don't thank me quite yet," Jim warned, "Not until I get to the bottom of this."

* * *

Bullet for a Ranger

As he'd suspected it would be, Jim's visit to Marshal Walt Castle was unproductive. The town lawman was uncooperative, in fact downright belligerent. The few records he'd provided had scant information. However, they did show that Castle had done nothing to try and apprehend the men behind the attacks on the citizens of Quitaque.

Upon leaving Castle's office, Jim went to Charlie's Barber Shop for a much-needed haircut, shave, and bath. Refreshed, he had dinner in the hotel restaurant, then obtained the information he'd requested from John Baker. He spent the rest of the day in his room, going over the report.

After supper, Jim headed for the Quicksilver Saloon. By now, Duke Ballantine would have had time to digest the news a Ranger was in town. It would be interesting to see his reaction. Jim placed a bullet in the empty chamber of his Colt and made sure the gun was loose in its holster before he entered the saloon.

From just inside the batwings, Jim scanned the room to see if Joe Hardy or any of his men were present. Several men at the bar turned to look at him, their gazes settling on the Ranger badge pinned to his vest. None of them were members of Hardy's bunch, nor were any of the gamblers at the tables. Unable to meet the stare of Jim's glittering blue eyes, the customers turned back to their drinks. Jim crossed the room and bellied up to the bar, finding a spot between two cowboys. One of the saloon women, a buxom brunette, smiled at the rugged Ranger. Jim nodded in return. Tom Doyle, the middle-aged bartender, fixed Jim with a worried glance. It was clear the man would rather be anywhere but here at this moment.

"Can I get you something, Ranger?" he asked.

"Sure," Jim answered. "Sarsaparilla, or if you don't have that, milk."

"Am I hearin' you right, Ranger?" Doyle questioned. "You don't want whiskey, or at least a beer?"

"Nope. Never touch alcohol. It dulls the senses, and in my line of work I can't afford that, so I'd appreciate it if you'd get me either a bottle of pop or a glass of milk."

"All right." Doyle rummaged under the bar and came up with two bottles of sarsaparilla. He placed them in front of Jim, uncorked one, and set a glass alongside that.

"That'll be ten cents, Ranger. Is there anything else you'll need?"

Jim tossed a dime on the bar.

"Yeah. If your boss is here, tell him Ranger Jim Blawcyzk wants to talk with him."

"Mister Ballantine? He's here, but I don't know if he can be disturbed," Doyle answered.

"He'll see me, one way or another," Jim replied. He placed his hand on the butt of his Peacemaker for emphasis.

Doyle swallowed, hard. Moisture appeared on his salt and pepper chevron moustache.

"All right, Ranger. I'll tell Mister Ballantine you're lookin' for him."

Doyle called to his assistant to cover for him, then

crossed the room and knocked on a door labeled "Private". The door opened, and Doyle had a brief, animated conversation with the person who'd answered. A moment later, that man trailed Doyle to the bar. He greeted Jim in a not unfriendly manner.

"Ranger, I'm Duke Ballantine. I understand you wish to speak with me."

"I do. If it's not too much trouble, Mister Ballantine, is there somewhere we can speak privately?" Jim answered.

"Of course. Step into my office. Bring your drink along. I'll make sure we aren't disturbed."

"Thank you." Jim picked up his bottles and glass, then followed Ballantine to his office. When the door closed behind them, Ballantine gestured to a chair opposite his desk. Another closed door was just behind that chair.

"Please, make yourself comfortable, Ranger...?"

"Blawcyzk," Jim supplied.

"Ranger Blawcyzk."

"Thank you." Jim picked up the chair and moved it to the opposite corner, where he could keep an eye on both doors.

"I see you're a cautious man, Ranger," Ballantine noted.

"It comes with the territory," Jim shrugged.

"I understand. However, I assure you that you have nothing to fear from me."

"That's not what I've been told," Jim answered. "But I want to hear what you have to say for yourself. I don't jump to conclusions, and always try to get both sides of a story. I assure you my investigation will be thorough, but impartial."

"That's very commendable. Pardon me while I pour myself a drink and light a smoke. Then I'll answer all of your questions."

"Certainly."

Jim studied Ballantine while the Quicksilver's owner filled a tumbler with rye, then lit a thin cigar. Ballantine was in his late thirties, tall and slender, with dark brown eyes, his black hair combed carefully in place. He was very good-looking, with even features and a ready smile. Dressed in a dark suit, he appeared very much a successful businessman.

"Now, Ranger, what did you wish to know?" Ballantine asked, after taking a swallow of his drink.

"First, I'm sure you're aware of the problems some of the businessmen in town have been facin'."

"I am," Ballantine replied.

"A lot of folks seem convinced you're the person responsible. They claim the trouble started shortly after you arrived."

"That's ridiculous. I'm trying to make a living just like everyone else," Ballantine protested.

"Nonetheless, you haven't been bothered by any threats, from what I've been told."

"That's true," Ballantine conceded, "However, I'm certain that's because I keep several men in my employ for protection. Running a saloon and gambling halls can be dangerous."

"And houses of ill repute?"

"I have an interest in those, yes. Obviously, you can see why I must be careful."

"Joe Hardy and his men work for you," Jim stated.

"That's right, they do. I need men I can depend on when it comes to a fight."

"Does that include having Hardy and his men attack a farmer and his family, just for patronizing John Baker's store?"

Ballantine sighed deeply.

"It's a bit hard to explain, but that should never have happened."

"Go on," Jim urged.

"Obviously, as a new businessman in Quitaque, I want to succeed. To do that, I must encourage people to patronize my establishments, instead of my competitors. I made the mistake of offering Joe a bonus for each customer he convinced to frequent my businesses, rather than the competition. I'm afraid he went too far in his methods of persuasion. He's been reprimanded, and warned if another such incident happens he will be fired. Besides, after the beating you handed Hardy and his men, I'm sure he won't be overly eager to start a fight again."

Ballantine paused, and pointed his cigar at Jim.

"Of course, if you'd identified yourself as a Ranger right off, rather than jumping into that fight, Joe would have stopped fighting immediately," he stated. "He knows I have no tolerance for anyone who doesn't respect the law. I can't afford to have my reputation besmirched by even the appearance of associating with outlaws."

"I'm sure you can't," Jim sarcastically answered. "And you're right, I should have identified myself as a Ranger. However, there wasn't time to do so. I was also hoping to remain incognito, so I could do some investigating on the quiet. You do realize if Hardy gets into trouble again, I'll arrest him."

"I'd expect nothing less," Ballantine answered.

"That brings us to the marshal," Jim said. "I've been told the town hired Walt Castle at your urging. From what I've determined, he doesn't seem to have done much to find whoever's stirrin' up trouble. He also threatened me, even after he knew I was a Ranger."

Again, Ballantine sighed.

"I did recommend Castle, yes. I knew him from up in Wichita, where I was a partner in a saloon, and where he was a town deputy. After three men were killed here, then Marshal Tuttle resigned, I felt Castle would be the right man for the job. However, I may have been mistaken. While Walt's a good man with a gun, I'm afraid he's not very bright. He hasn't even been able to begin to discover who's responsible for those killings, or any other crimes. He has managed to arrest a few drunken cowpunchers, but that's about all. As far as his alleged threats against you, I'd say that's merely professional jealousy."

"I wish I could be as certain as you are about that," Jim answered.

"I'll speak to the marshal, and make sure he understands why you're here, Ranger," Ballantine offered. "He'll listen to me."

"*Bueno,*" Jim answered. "Make sure Hardy and his men understand what'll happen to 'em if they cross me again, too."

"I'll do that," Ballantine promised. He glanced at the Regulator clock on the wall behind his desk.

"I really need to get on the floor, so unless you have any further questions I'd appreciate ending this discussion," he said.

"I'm done for now," Jim answered. "If I need to talk with you again, I'll find you."

"That won't be hard. I'm here every night," Ballantine answered. "Now, please feel free to stay and enjoy the hospitality of the Quicksilver. Your drinks are on the house, of course."

"I appreciate your offer, Mister Ballantine," Jim replied. "However, as I told John Baker when he offered me a free room and meals at his hotel, I have to avoid the slightest hint that I'm showing favoritism, or worse, taking a bribe. I will stay for a few more sarsaparillas, but I'll pay for them."

"I understand," Ballantine repeated. "Is there anything else I can do for you?"

"Just one thing," Jim replied. "I enjoy a good game of poker. I'd like to sit in on one, if there's a place available."

"I'll tell Jess Henderson, my chief houseman, to set you up. I assure you all the games here are honest."

"I'm certain they are. I also want to thank you for being so cooperative, Mister Ballantine."

"I'm always willing to help the law," Ballantine smiled.

* * *

Jim was having supper, as usual, in the Panhandle Plaza's restaurant. He'd downed a large steak, potatoes, and green beans, topping that off with a slab of apple pie and two cups of coffee. Now, his meal finished, he was feeling slightly feverish. His face was flushed, and nausea roiled his guts.

Penelope, his waitress, returned, with the coffee pot in her hand.

"Another cup of coffee, Ranger Blawcyzk?" she asked.

"No thanks," Jim replied. "I'm feelin' kinda funny."

He brushed the back of his hand across his forehead. It came away dripping with sweat.

"You do look kind of poorly," Penelope agreed.

"Perhaps you need to lie down for a bit."

"I reckon you're right," Jim agreed. He attempted to push back from the table. Instead, he slumped over in his chair, his head dropping alongside his empty plate.

"Ranger!" Penny shook his shoulder. "Ranger!"

Jim managed to lift his head.

"Huh?"

"You fainted, Ranger. Let me get you some water, then I'll have Mister Baker help you to your room," Penelope offered.

"No, thanks just the same. That's not necessary. I'll be fine once I get some rest. I'm just a bit dizzy, that's all."

Jim slid back his chair and stood up, wobbling slightly.

"Are you sure?" Penelope asked. "Perhaps you should see Doctor Simpson."

"I'm all right," Jim insisted. "I just ate too much, that's all. I'll step outside for some air. That'll take care of this."

"If you're certain, Ranger," Penelope dubiously answered.

"I am. I'll see you tomorrow, Penny."

Jim weaved his way out of the dining room and stumbled down the stairs. Mind fogged, he started uncertainly toward the Horse Heaven. When he reached the alley alongside the hotel, several pairs of hands grabbed him and dragged him into the narrow, unlit pathway.

"You look pretty sick, Ranger," a voice muttered. "Come with us. We'll get you some help."

"Thanks. Reckon I'd..." Jim's voice trailed off, and he collapsed to the dirt. The next thing he'd remember would be waking up in a strange room alongside a dead saloon woman... a woman who'd been killed with his knife.

Chapter Four

JIM WAS still lying on the bunk when the marshal returned, accompanied by Duke Ballantine and Joe Hardy. The Ranger sat up, his head whirling from the effort.

"I've brought you breakfast, Ranger," Castle announced. He kept his pistol trained on Jim while he unlocked the door, placed a covered tray on the floor, and slid it into the cell. "Enjoy it. You don't have many more comin'."

"I'm not hungry," Jim answered.

"I wouldn't imagine you are," Ballantine said, "You must have a wicked hangover from all the liquor you consumed last night."

"You know I don't drink. Besides, I wasn't even in your place last night, Ballantine," Jim answered.

"Sure you were. Joe and I both saw you. So did a lot of others. Isn't that right, Joe?"

"It sure is," Hardy said, grinning wickedly. "You got real liquored-up, Ranger. Boy howdy, you're an awfully mean drunk. I warned Jenny not to take you upstairs, but she wouldn't listen. Now she's dead, and you're gonna hang. I'll even volunteer to put the noose around your neck."

"I'm surprised I haven't been lynched already," Jim snapped.

"That won't happen, Ranger," Ballantine said. "You see, if you were to be hung by a lynch mob, that would undoubtedly bring an investigation by Austin. No, I've convinced the town to wait for the circuit judge, who is due in ten days or so. You'll be tried and executed, properly and legally."

"You won't get away with this, Ballantine," Jim warned.

"I'm not the person who killed Jenny," Ballantine retorted. "I'm just a citizen attempting to make certain justice is done. Of course, I also have a personal interest in this case, since it was one of my valued employees you murdered."

Despite his headache, Jim leapt to his feet.

"Ballantine, you miserable liar," he shouted. "When I get my hands on you..."

"Don't make threats like that, Ranger," Marshal Castle advised, "Or I'll handcuff you to the bunk."

"That won't be necessary, Marshal," Ballantine said. "I'm leaving now. You see, I have to make the funeral arrangements for poor Jenny Cole."

Ballantine sniffled, and pulled a handkerchief from his breast pocket. He dabbed at his eyes.

"I... I'm sorry," he mumbled. "It's just... losing Jenny like this."

"Don't worry, Duke," Hardy said, "This so-called lawman'll pay for what he did. We'll see to that." He put an arm around Ballantine's shoulders and led him outside.

"It's a good thing Mister Ballantine insisted you be tried for killin' Jenny, Ranger, or I'd head a lynch party myself," Castle snarled. "Even hangin's better'n you deserve."

Jim didn't give Castle the satisfaction of a reply. He merely dropped back onto his bunk, face-down. The marshal glared at Jim's back for several minutes, then turned away in disgust.

* * *

An hour later, John Baker burst through the marshal's door. He stalked up to Castle and jabbed a finger into his chest.

"Marshal, I understand you've arrested Ranger Blawcyzk. I want to see him," Baker demanded.

"No one can talk to him before the trial," Castle replied.

"Either I talk to him right now, or I'll wire Austin requesting to have more Rangers sent up here to take over enforcing the law in this town," Baker insisted. "I'm sure you wouldn't want that."

"No, I reckon not," Castle conceded. "All right. You can see the Ranger, but only for a few minutes."

"That's all the time I'll need," Baker answered.

Castle lifted his keys from a wall peg, and led Baker through the thick oak door which separated the jail's lone cell from his office.

"You've got company, Ranger," he said. Castle unlocked the cell, let Baker in, then relocked the door.

"Ten minutes," he ordered.

Baker waited until Castle returned to his office.

"Lieutenant, I came as soon as I heard. What happened?"

"Thanks for comin', Mister Baker. I don't rightly know," Jim answered. "Last I remember was eatin' supper, then gettin' real sick. Next thing I know, I'm in a room over the Quicksilver, in bed with one of Ballantine's women. And she's dead, with my knife stuck in her chest."

"You didn't kill her, of course."

"Of course not. But someone's sure gone to an awful lot of trouble to make certain it looks like I did."

"Duke Ballantine."

"Seems that way. Someone must've slipped me something to knock me out. However, I wasn't even in the Quicksilver last night. In fact, I had supper at your hotel."

"You're not saying that I could do something like this?" Baker objected.

"No I'm not, at least not yet," Jim told him. "Although if I was given something, it had to be in my food or coffee at your place. Please, keep quiet about that for now."

"I won't say anything, if that's what you want," Baker assured him. "I've got to help you somehow. What can I do?"

"I appreciate that. There are a couple of things you can do for me."

"What are they?"

"First, try'n get the rest of my clothes from the Quicksilver and bring them to me. As you no doubt noticed, I was run outta there wearin' only my levis."

"Done. What else?"

"Send a wire to Captain Trumbull at Ranger Headquarters. Let him know what's happened, and tell him to send another Ranger up here pronto. Ask him for Smoky McCue or Jim Huggins if either one's available."

"Of course. Anything further?"

"Yeah. Let Chauncey Brennan know what's happened. Tell him to take care of my horses until I'm outta this fix."

"I'll make sure he does. Is that all?"

"There's one more thing. Can you have one of the priests from the Catholic mission visit me?"

"Certainly. I'll send that telegram, then bring your clothes. After that I'll see Brennan and the priest."

"Thanks."

Castle stuck his head through the door.

"Two more minutes."

"We're finished," Baker answered. "Unlock the cell, Marshal."

Castle did as told. Baker paused outside Jim's cell.

"Are you certain that's everything you need?" he asked.

"For now," Jim answered.

"All right. I'll check in later, so if you think of anything else let me know then."

"I will, and I appreciate your help," Jim said.

"Out, Baker," Castle snapped.

Once Baker had left, Jim sat on the edge of his bunk. He needed, somehow, to find proof against Duke Ballantine, or whoever had framed him for murder. And right now, it looked like he'd have to do that from inside a locked cell.

With a sigh of frustration, Jim stretched out on his back on the thin mattress, hands behind his head. True, Duke Ballantine was the most obvious suspect. But Jim hadn't been in the Quicksilver, nor seen Ballantine or any of his cronies, for the past three days. Additionally, he'd only eaten in the Panhandle Plaza's dining room. Whatever drug he'd been slipped had to have been administered through his supper by someone at the hotel. Had they been paid to do so by Duke Ballantine? Or, despite all his attempts to appear an upright citizen seeking Ranger assistance, was John Baker instead behind the problems in Quitaque, and the man who'd framed Jim? Throwing suspicion on Ballantine would be the ideal method to keep the spotlight off Baker. After all, what better way would there be for Baker to take suspicion off himself and eliminate a rival than by having the Texas Rangers do his dirty work? There was even the possibility Ballantine and Baker were working together, with Baker playing the role of the besieged honest businessman. Perhaps the two were conspiring to drive the rest of Quitaque's merchants out of business, then sharing the spoils.

Of course, none of that mattered unless Jim found a way out of this fix, and quickly. By now the whole town knew that he'd been found in bed alongside a dead saloon woman. A woman who'd been murdered, with his knife in her chest. Whoever wanted him dead would be sure to keep stirring the pot, making certain the lurid details of Jenny Cole's death were repeated, the story growing more exaggerated and gruesome with each retelling. By tomorrow at the latest, practically every resident of Quitaque would be convinced of Jim's guilt. Even the society matrons, who otherwise wouldn't be caught dead acknowledging a saloon entertainer like Jenny Cole, would be clamoring for the Ranger's hanging.

Jim spent the better part of an hour puzzling things out. His thoughts were disturbed when the sounds of an argument came through the thick oak door separating the cell from the marshal's office. A moment later, the door swung open. John Baker stood there, along with an infuriated Marshal Castle. Baker carried the rest of Jim's clothes.

"I've agreed to let you speak with the prisoner once more, but five minutes is all," Castle ordered.

"That's more than sufficient," Baker responded. "Now close that door."

"All right."

Baker waited until the door was shut before speaking again.

"Bet you were wonderin' if I'd come back, Lieutenant," he said.

"Not really," Jim answered. "I trust you, Mister Baker." He knew, even if Baker was behind the plot to frame him, the man would need to maintain a facade of innocence. That meant Jim would need to play along to have any chance of tripping Baker up.

"I've brought your clothes," Baker continued. He slid the garments under the bars. "It took some doin'," he added, as Jim picked up his boots and socks, then sat on the edge of the bunk to pull them on. "Ballantine didn't want to give them up. I had to convince him that I'm also beginning to think you're guilty of murder. I told him it'd look better to a jury if they didn't hear how you'd been kept half-naked in a dingy cell for days. That made up his mind. Of course, it's preposterous to even consider you murdered that gal, but it was the only argument which Ballantine would buy."

"Don't apologize," Jim said, as he shrugged into his shirt. "It worked, didn't it?"

"Yeah, that's right," Baker agreed. "It did."

"That's all that matters. What about everything else?"

"All set. Your request went to Austin. I'll check for a reply every so often."

"Don't bother. Cap'n Trumbull won't send one, since that would telegraph his plans, if you'll pardon the pun. He'll just send a man here."

"Then I'll watch for another Ranger to arrive. Now, as for your horses, Chauncey promised to care for them as long as necessary. He said don't worry about the money. He also said they'd get a peppermint every day."

"Good. That's a big worry off my mind."

"This will also ease your mind some. Father Campos said he'll come by to visit with you tomorrow morning, right after Mass."

"Thanks, Mister Baker. I appreciate you goin' to all this trouble.

"Pshaw! It's no bother at all," Baker answered. "I'm also trying to find you an attorney."

"You needn't. Anything that needs to be said I can say myself. Besides, it'd be a fool's errand," Jim answered. "I'm already tried, convicted, and hung. It's just a matter of goin' through the motions of a trial."

"You mean you're givin' up?"

"Not at all. I'm gonna find a way out of this mess, bet a hat on it," Jim answered, with a rueful grin. "I don't look good wearin' a hemp necktie."

The door opened, and Marshal Castle poked his head into the hallway.

"Time's up, Baker," he ordered.

"All right, Marshal," Baker replied. "Ranger, I'll check back with you tomorrow afternoon."

"All right. And thanks again," Jim answered.

After Baker had departed, Jim once again stretched out on the mattress. Somewhere in Quitaque was the answer he needed. He just had to find it.

Chapter Five

JIM HAD finished breakfast and was pacing the floor of his cell, working off tension and stretching his cramped muscles, when the corridor door opened. Marshal Castle was there, accompanied by a brown-robed Franciscan.

"Got a padre here says you want to see him," Castle stated. "I reckon it'll be all right, as long as you don't take too much time."

"I'll visit with this man as long as he wants... or as I'd like, Marshal", the priest answered in a soft voice, but one edged with steel. "And please, once I am in the cell, shut this door behind you. Our talk must be private. Since your prisoner may be facing a death sentence, I will be offering him the Sacrament of Penance. His cell will be a confessional. That means any sins which he may reveal are subject to the seal of the confessional. When he makes his confession, it is between himself, God, and myself as God's representative. I can divulge nothing about what is said, and I must make certain we are not overheard."

"All right, padre," Castle agreed. "I reckon he won't tell you anything we don't already know. Just give a holler when you're through."

Castle unlocked the cell door to admit the priest, then relocked it and departed, closing the outer door behind him.

"Shh. Just a moment," the priest warned Jim. He listened carefully, until he was satisfied Castle wasn't standing with his ear pressed to the door. He then checked the cell's single, barred window to be sure Castle wasn't hovering outside, eavesdropping.

"All right. I believe it's safe, but let's keep our conversation soft, just to make certain. I'm Father Miguel Campos."

"Jim Blawcyzk. Thanks for coming, Father."

"I'm happy to accommodate your request. I understand you are a Texas Ranger."

"That's right, Father. I have been for quite a few years."

"However, now you are accused of a heinous crime. You were found in bed with a soiled dove, to use a polite term. And that woman had been murdered."

"That's correct, Father, but I didn't kill her. I didn't have any relations with her, either. I have sins I wish to confess, but murder and adultery are not among them."

"Would you like to talk about it?"

"I certainly would, Father. I sure need to talk to

someone who'll listen to me."

"Then let's do that first. Once we are finished, I'll hear your Confession."

"That's not a bad idea," Jim agreed.

"Fine. Let's start."

"All right. Father, I was sent here to investigate apparent attempts to drive legitimate businesses out of Quitaque, and of course the murders of three men. My investigation has pointed to one individual as the most likely suspect. I'd rather not divulge his name at this point."

"That's not necessary," Father Campos agreed. "Go on."

"I believe I made that person, or whoever is behind this trouble, worried that I was getting close to having enough evidence to convict him, so he decided he had to get rid of me. As far as I can figure, somehow he managed to have someone slip a drug into my supper the night before last. Just after eating, I got real sick. The next thing I remember was waking up in a strange room, with the dead woman next to me. My head hurt so badly I couldn't think straight, but I know I didn't kill that woman. In fact, I'd only seen her once before, briefly in passing."

"If what you say is true, why didn't that person just have you shot from ambush?" the priest asked.

"Most likely because he realized killin' a Ranger would only bring more here," Jim answered. "But having me tried, convicted, and hung for murder would solve that dilemma."

"I see," Father Campos replied. "Pardon me if I play

devil's advocate for a bit. You claim you didn't kill the woman. I believe you, but are you certain you didn't commit adultery with her? After all, a man on the trail for a long time, then virtually alone in a strange town, might well succumb to temptation. You were at the saloon, had a few drinks, and one thing led to another."

"No Father, I did not," Jim reiterated. "I don't drink liquor, not even beer, and I've been a happily married man for years. I've got my wife and a teenaged son. I could never be unfaithful to Julia, and I sure couldn't tell Charlie not to go to bed with a woman if I didn't practice what *I* preached. What kind of father would that make me?"

"I understand. So apparently you were drugged, brought to that room, and left there with the woman."

"Who was killed with my knife," Jim added. "Whoever wants me dead did a fine job of settin' me up. If I were on the jury, even I'd have to vote to convict myself, the evidence is so good."

"Try not to lose faith. I'm certain justice will be done, somehow."

"I hope you're right, Father."

"Keep your faith in the Lord, Jim," the priest advised. "His will shall be done."

"I'll do my best, Father, but sometimes that ain't easy."

"I know that. Now, before our friend the marshal becomes impatient, perhaps I should hear your Confession."

"All right, Father."

"I'll be ready in a moment."

Father Campos placed a purple stole around his shoulders. When he took a seat on one end of the bunk, Jim knelt on the rock floor.

"Whenever you wish to start, Jim."

"Bless me Father, for I have sinned..." Jim began, crossing himself. He went through the ritual of the Sacrament of Penance, recalling his sins since his last Confession, reciting the Act of Contrition, then receiving absolution and penance from the priest. Finally, Father Campos blessed him to conclude the sacrament.

"Thank you, Father." Jim repeated the traditional ending.

"I didn't bring the Host with me today, since I wasn't positive you'd want to say Confession and receive Communion," Father Campos explained. "Unfortunately, I will be away for the next two days, visiting parishioners at some outlying ranches. I'll return after that so you may receive Holy Eucharist."

"I'll appreciate that, Father," Jim answered. "I also have one more request."

"What is that?"

"If for some reason I don't make it outta here, could you be sure and get in touch with my wife and son? Let them know whatever they might hear isn't true."

"Of course. How would I get in touch with them?"

"You could send a letter in care of Ranger

Headquarters, or better still, to Julia Blawcyzk, at the JB Bar Ranch in San Leanna."

"I'll do that," the priest promised. "However, let's not be premature. I'm also certain your wife and son would realize the truth in any event. Don't sell them short."

"All right. I'll take your advice," Jim agreed.

"Good. Now I'd better call the marshal. I don't want him to have any excuse to bar my visits," Father Campos said. "I'll also keep my eyes and ears open. You'd be surprised what a priest hears. I might learn something useful."

"I'm grateful for that, too," Jim said.

"Good." Campos turned to the cell door.

"Marshal Castle!" he called. A moment later, the outer door opened.

"You're ready to leave, padre?" Castle asked.

"Yes, I am. I'll return in three days for another visit."

"Did this hombre admit to killin' Jenny Cole?" Castle asked.

"As I told you, I cannot reveal anything said to me during Confession," Father Campos answered.

"Mebbe I'll have to make you talk," the marshal threatened.

"You could torture me, even kill me, but you could not get me to break my solemn vows," the priest insisted. "I would never violate the seal of the confessional. Now, let me out."

"All right." Castle unlocked the cell door, then stood aside.

"Jim, keep praying that justice will be done," Father Campos advised. "The Lord will hear you."

"I will. And thanks again, Father. Adios."

"Adios, Lieutenant."

Once the priest had departed, Castle turned back to Jim.

"You can pray all you want," he snarled, "but instead of seein' the Pearly Gates, you'll be meetin' up with the devil real soon."

"We'll just have to wait and see, won't we, Marshal?" Jim retorted.

Castle didn't reply. He turned and went to his office, slamming the door shut behind him.

* * *

Later that afternoon, Duke Ballantine put in an appearance at the jail.

"I understand you had a visit from one of the priests at the mission, Ranger," he said.

"That's right," Jim admitted. "What difference does that make to you?"

"It doesn't mean a thing to me," Ballantine answered.

"But it was a right smart move on your part. If I knew I'd be facin' a hang rope in a few days, I'd want to see a preacher too. After all, confession is good for the soul. I hope you feel better, telling that priest you murdered Jenny Cole."

"I hate to disappoint you, but I didn't admit to that, because it isn't true. You know that, Ballantine. If I were you, I'd start thinking about seeing that preacher yourself, because I'm gonna prove you were behind that killing."

"You'll be dead before you ever get the chance," Ballantine replied. "The circuit judge'll be arriving in less than a week now. Once he's here, we'll have your trial. It wouldn't surprise me a bit if you're hung the same day. Think about that."

Ballantine spun on his heel and stalked out of the jail before Jim could reply.

* * *

That night, as usual, Jim said his evening prayers, lying on the bunk. He had taken to concluding them with the Rosary, despite not having a set of beads. He kept track of the decades by counting the Hail Marys, Glory Bes, and Our Fathers in his head.

In spite of Father Campos' visit and his prayers, Jim was extremely restless so sleep was long in coming. The night was hot and muggy, with not a breeze stirring. The stuffy cell only exacerbated the heat and humidity.

Jim had stripped down to his jeans, but sweat still covered his forehead and upper torso. His thick blonde hair was matted down with perspiration.

"I'm sure missin' Julia and Charlie," he whispered, half-aloud. "Wish I was with them right now. I don't much care what happens to me, but I hate the thought of what it'll do to them, when people say I was a lowdown, cheatin' murderer. That'll break Julia's heart, and it'll just about tear Charlie apart."

Jim sighed.

"I reckon my only chance right now is that Smoky, or whoever Cap'n Trumbull might send up here, arrives before that judge. Smoke'd have to work real fast once he got here. He'd have to come up with the real killer before my trial. And that's assumin' Baker even sent my message at all. If he's behind all this, or is in cahoots with Ballantine, then he never sent that wire. I'd bet a hat on that. Baker and Ballantine. Sounds like a sleazy law firm, or mebbe a couple of accountants," he ruefully chuckled. "But they might just be the hombres who place a noose around my neck."

Jim sat up, picked up his shirt from the floor, wiped sweat from his face and chest, then settled back with a grunt. For over an hour he tossed restlessly, until sleep finally overcame the exhausted Ranger.

"Julia," Jim moaned. His petite wife appeared, running across a bluebonnet covered field toward him. As always, her brown eyes sparkled with joy. Her long, brunette tresses flowed in the wind like a silken waterfall.

"Dad!" From the opposite direction, Charlie called. Jim's teenaged son was mounted on his pet buckskin paint gelding, Ted. Charlie admired his lawman father, and his one ambition in life was to become a Texas Ranger, just like Jim. His tow hair stuck out from under his battered Stetson. Charlie's blue eyes, so much like his father's, fixed Jim with an angry stare.

"Charlie! No!" Jim shouted, when his son leveled a Winchester at him. "Don't!"

"You'll never hurt Mom again!" Charlie screamed. He levered the rifle and fired. Jim buckled at the impact of a heavy bullet ripping into his belly.

"But Charlie! I didn't..." Jim cried, to no avail. Charlie fired again and again, his bullets ripping through Jim's guts, until the rifle's chamber was emptied. Jim pitched to the dirt.

Julia now stood over her husband.

"Julia, you believe me, don't you?" Jim gasped.

"Certainly I do, my darling husband."

Julia laughed evilly. Her eyes glared red. She pulled a knife from inside her dress, raised it high above her head, and plunged it into Jim's chest. Over and over she thrust that blade into his heart.

Next Smoky McCue, Sergeant Jim Huggins, and Captain Trumbull appeared. McCue and Huggins emptied their six-guns into Jim's still-twitching corpse. When they had finished, Trumbull bent over the body and ripped Jim's badge from his chest.

McCue's and Huggins' visages gradually changed, dissolving into John Baker and Duke Ballantine. The two Quitaque saloon men laughed harshly. Their faces were red, with thin goatees and mustaches. Horns protruded from their heads.

"Get up, Blawcyzk!" they ordered, prodding the now-naked Ranger with pitchforks. Jim's belly was riddled with bullet holes, his chest shredded by knife slashes. Blood coated his entire body.

"Get up!" Baker ordered again. He jabbed his pitchfork into Jim's ribs. Jim struggled to his feet.

"Welcome to your new home, Ranger," Ballantine smirked. "They say Texas in the summer is hotter than Hell. You're about to find out that isn't true."

He stabbed Jim in the back with his pitchfork, pushing him toward a fiery pit. Jim stumbled toward the flames. When he hesitated at the rim of the crevasse, Ballantine and Baker jabbed him again, shoving him into the pit. Jim spiraled down into a bottomless abyss of smoke and fire.

Jim awoke with a scream. He jerked upright, his heart pounding. He was drenched with sweat, and struggled for breath.

"It was only a nightmare," he tried to tell himself. "Just a bad dream, that's all."

Gradually, Jim's heart rate returned to its normal rhythm. His breathing came more easily. Finally, he settled back onto the bunk.

Jim closed his eyes, trying to force himself to relax. However, sleep would not return this night. His jangled nerves would not permit it.

Chapter Six

JIM SPENT the next several days chafing at his confinement. He was accustomed to being on the trail, traveling through the wide open spaces of Texas, not confined behind bars. Even when he was home with his family, after a few days the desire to head out again became an overwhelming urge gnawing at his insides. He'd been born to wander, and could never stay in any one place for long. Being locked up in a tiny jail cell was tearing at the very fiber of his being. Compounding his frustration, there'd been no sign of Smoky McCue, Jim Huggins, or any other Ranger. Of course, it was really too soon to expect one of his fellow Rangers. Unless one happened to be somewhere in the area, and where he could receive a telegram, it was too far for any Ranger to reach Quitaque before Jim's trial. Most likely Jim would be tried, convicted, and hung before help could arrive from Austin. His only glimmer of hope was rapidly fading.

Adding to his torment, Jim had received no visitors since Father Campos left, except for that brief visit from Duke Ballantine. Marshal Castle delivered his meals, waited while Jim ate, then departed, usually without saying a word. Other than that, the Ranger had had no human contact at all. He had hoped Chauncey Brennan, or at least John Baker, would put in an appearance, but there had been no sign of either man.

"Of course, what do you expect?" Jim muttered to himself. "You're a killer in the eyes of everyone in town. Worse, a woman-killer. Even Baker and Chauncey probably believe that at this point. But I can't figure why Father Campos hasn't come by again."

It was now four days since the priest's visit. Father Campos hadn't come back with the Eucharist the previous day, as he'd promised. His failure to return was tearing at Jim's guts, more than anything else. Jim's question to Marshal Castle about whether he had heard from Father Campos elicited only a sneer and a disdainful laugh.

"I reckon even that padre doesn't want to be bothered with a no good jasper who killed a woman," Castle said.

When the corridor's door finally opened, about mid-morning, Jim eagerly leapt from his bunk, fully expecting to see the brown-robed Franciscan. Instead, Marshal Castle was there, again accompanied by Duke Ballantine.

"I should've figured it was you, Ballantine," Jim said. "Did you come to gloat again?"

"Not at all. I think it's tragic that your temper has put you in this situation, Lieutenant," Ballantine objected. "I'm sure you were a fine lawman up until now. No, I stopped by to let you know the circuit judge will arrive the day after tomorrow. He's scheduled your trial for eleven o'clock the next morning. Jury selection will be at ten. It'll soon be over for you. Finally Jenny Cole will be able to rest peacefully, knowing her murder has been avenged."

"Jenny's ghost'll be wanderin' around here for a long time, since her real killer will still be on the loose," Jim answered. "You might remember that, Ballantine. In fact, mebbe we'll both haunt you."

"Nice try, Lieutenant. However, I don't believe in supernatural spirits, so your threat doesn't frighten me one bit. I must admit, I am looking forward to your trial and hanging."

"Just don't expect the satisfaction of seein' me beg for mercy," Jim retorted.

"Of course not," Ballantine said. "Hasta la vista, Ranger."

In frustration, Jim took his empty tin cup and threw it at the oak door, once it shut behind the Quicksilver's owner. The mug bounced off the door and clattered to the floor.

"Well, that was useless," Jim scolded himself, while he watched the cup spin under a ladder-backed chair. "You're gonna lose it if you're not careful, Ranger."

In despair, Jim dropped back onto his mattress. After an hour he drifted into a fitful sleep. His nap was interrupted when the door swung open once again. This time, Father Campos stood alongside the marshal. He carried a small, golden pyx.

Chapter Six 73

"Father!" Jim jumped from the bunk.

"Hello, Jim," Father Campos smiled. "As promised, I've brought you Communion. I apologize for being delayed. Betty Malone, out at the Rocking M Ranch, went into labor shortly after I arrived there. She was having a difficult birth. Twins. I remained with Betty and her husband Frank until I was certain everyone would be all right. I'm happy to say Betty gave birth to a healthy boy and girl. I baptized them Katherine and Gregory. They'll join three brothers and four sisters. But by the time it was apparent Betty and the newborns were going to be fine, it was long after dark. I decided to stay overnight, then return to town this morning."

"I certainly understand, and that doesn't matter, Father. I'm just grateful to see you," Jim responded.

"Nevertheless, my delay must have given you reason for concern," the priest replied. "Marshal, if you would open the cell."

"Just a minute, padre," Castle ordered. "What've you got inside that little gold dish? I need to see it."

"This pyx contains the consecrated Host, the Body of Our Lord Jesus Christ," Father Campos replied. "Jim, Lieutenant Blawcyzk, wishes to receive the Lord in Holy Communion. Certainly you don't think I have a loaded pistol inside this vessel, Marshal?"

"Of course not," Castle answered. "But you might have some poison in there. Mebbe the Ranger asked you to bring him somethin' so he could cheat the gallows."

The priest gave Castle a withering look.

Chapter Six

Bullet for a Ranger

"Marshal, if I assisted Lieutenant Blawcyzk, or anyone else, to commit suicide it would be a mortal sin in the eyes of God. Now if you would please leave us alone, I am ready to administer the Sacrament."

"All right," the marshal conceded. He opened Jim's cell to admit the priest, relocked it, then went to his office, but left the outer door slightly ajar.

"Jim, how are you holding up?" Father Campos asked.

"About as well as can be expected, I guess," Jim shrugged. "I'm just kinda surprised I haven't heard from Captain Trumbull, or that one of my pardners hasn't shown up. John Baker hasn't even been by. But now that you're here, I feel a lot better."

"So you haven't given up hope? That's good."

"Not yet. But it is gettin' harder to keep my spirits up."

"That's another reason for you to receive Communion," Father Campos said. "It will give you the strength and courage needed to face your travails. Are you ready for me to proceed now?"

"I am, Father."

"Fine."

Jim knelt on the hard rock floor and bowed his head.

Father Campos opened the pyx and removed the consecrated Host. He held it aloft.

"*Ecce Agnus Dei, ecce qui tollit peccata mundi,*" he intoned.

"*Domine, non sum dignus et intres sub tectum meum, sed tantum dic verbo, et anabitur anima mea,*" Jim replied. The words and response were repeated three times. Then Jim lifted his head and opened his mouth to receive the Body of Christ.

"*Corpus Domini nostri Jesu Christi custodiat animam tuam in vitam aeternam,*" Father Campos recited, as he placed the Host on Jim's tongue.

"*Amen.*" Jim said. He made the Sign of the Cross, then remained kneeling for a few moments, silently praying. He crossed himself again, then came to his feet.

"Thank you, Father," he said. "Will you be able to visit again before the trial?"

"Of course, Jim," the priest replied. "I'll also be with you during the trial, and afterwards."

"I'm grateful for that."

Father Campos glanced at the partially open outer door. He maneuvered so his back was to that door, effectively blocking the marshal's view of the cell. He lowered his voice.

"Jim, you'll recall I told you I would keep my eyes and ears open, and that a priest often hears things, things which might not be confided to a lay person," he said.

"I do," Jim answered.

"Good. There has been a lot of talk around town of a lynching. That's pretty much died down. However, apparently, from what I have learned, Duke Ballantine is concerned the Rangers might still show up before your trial, or that somehow you might be found innocent. Rumors are circulating that you'll never come to trial. Ballantine doesn't intend for you to leave Quitaque alive."

"So Ballantine is the man behind all this," Jim hissed.

"Evidently, but there's still no proof of that, or that he's working alone. I'm just repeating what I have heard."

"What are Ballantine's plans, if he doesn't intend to wait for that trial?" Jim questioned.

"You're to be shot and killed attempting to escape," Father Campos explained. "I hope to prevent that. Here. Take this."

The priest reached inside his robes and came up with a long, thin-bladed knife. He passed it to Jim. The Ranger looked at it in disbelief, then slid it inside his shirt.

"I couldn't smuggle a pistol to you, so that knife will have to do," Father Campos explained. "I sincerely hope you won't have to use it, but if you do, use it well. This is one of those circumstances where violence, even killing if necessary, is just in the eyes of the Church, and the Lord," he concluded. "Please be careful."

"I understand, Father," Jim answered. "But perhaps you should leave now. If Castle should somehow get suspicious, and discover the knife while you're still here..."

"I get the point," the priest replied.

"You just might, if Castle finds this knife."

"Ouch!" Father Campos winced at the horrific pun. "Confession again for you, Jim. Then seven Our Fathers and seven Hail Marys for your penance."

"I'm serious," Jim insisted. "What better way to make sure I'm hung than for the marshal to kill you with this knife, then blame that on me?"

"I see what you mean," Father Campos agreed. "I should leave. However, let's talk for a few more minutes. That will help you."

"If you're sure, Father," Jim replied.

"I am," Father Campos assured him.

The Ranger and priest talked for another twenty minutes. Finally satisfied he had done everything he could, Father Campos stood up.

"Now it really is time for me to go," he said. He raised his voice and called for the marshal.

"Marshal Castle. I'm through here."

Castle appeared in the doorway.

"It's about time," he muttered. He unlocked Jim's cell.

"Father, I'm grateful to you for everything," Jim said.

"Thank you," the priest replied. He raised his right hand to bless the Ranger.

"In nomine Patris, et Filii, et Spiritus Sancti. Amen."

"Thank you, Father."

"Jim, remember the Lord is always with you, even in your darkest hour. Never forget that," Father Campos advised. "And please, use the knowledge and gifts you have received wisely."

"I will," Jim assured him. He couldn't help but grin at the priest's thinly veiled reference to the knife now concealed inside his shirt.

"Good. I'll stop by again tomorrow," Father Campos promised.

"I'll be here," Jim chuckled.

"That's enough, you two. Padre, you've gotta leave," Castle insisted.

"All right, Marshal."

While Castle escorted the priest outside, Jim slipped the knife from inside his shirt, cut a slit in the side of his mattress which was against the wall, and slid the knife inside. He rubbed dirt on the cut, then draped a rumpled blanket over the side of the bunk. That done, he pulled off his shirt and boots, then stretched out on his belly in the bunk. When Castle looked in on him a few moments later, he was softly snoring, like a man deeply asleep.

* * *

About one o'clock the next morning, Jim was awakened by the opening of the hall door. A match flared, and the wall lamp was lit.

"Get up, Ranger," Marshal Castle ordered.

"Huh? What?" Jim mumbled. Despite being fully awake, he feigned the reaction of a man interrupted in the midst of a deep sleep.

"You heard me. Get up. And get dressed," Castle snapped.

"Are you crazy, Marshal? It's the middle of the night. Go away and let me sleep."

"Get outta that bunk before I drag you out," Castle answered.

"All right, all right. Give me a minute." Jim flopped around as if disoriented while he rummaged under his blanket, until he slid the knife Father Campos had given him from inside the mattress. He left it under the blanket while sat up, then pulled on his boots and socks. He shrugged into his shirt, then lay on his back once again. He slipped the knife from beneath the blanket and snugged it against his back, under the shirt.

"I said get up, you no-good s.o.b.," Castle cursed.

Jim came to his feet. He tied his bandanna around his neck and jammed his Stetson on his head.

"I'm up. What's the hurry, Marshal?" he questioned.

"It's time for you to break jail," Castle answered, as he unlocked the cell door. He held his six-gun leveled at the Ranger's chest.

"I'm not leavin' this cell. What in blue blazes are you talkin' about?" Jim demanded.

"It's simple. Duke doesn't want to take any chances

on a trial. There's always the possibility somethin' will go wrong and you'll be let go. So, you're gonna attempt to escape. Of course, you'll be shot and killed when you do. That's gonna be right now. Get movin'. You have to be out of that cell when I plug you, so it'll look like you tried to make a break for it."

"And when I do, you'll shoot me in the back," Jim stated.

"Of course," Castle replied. "The old Mexican 'Law of Flight', Ranger."

"What if I don't move? That'll spoil your plan, Marshal."

"Then I'll just drill you right through the guts, drag you out to the office, claim I shot you there when you broke out, and let you die real slow," Castle explained. "What's it gonna be? Make up your mind, quick."

"I reckon a bullet in the back's better'n a hangman's noose. It's quicker, too," Jim shrugged. "You win, Marshal. But first, can I ask you somethin' that's been botherin' me?"

"Make it quick."

"Why'd Duke have Jenny Cole killed? That's real low, killin' a woman just to frame me."

"I reckon it won't hurt to tell you," Castle replied. "There were a couple of reasons. Jenny was the most popular of Duke's girls. That went to her head, and she started pressin' him for more money. When he refused, she threatened to walk out on him. Duke couldn't stand for that. So, he figured to kill two birds with one stone. First, he got rid of Jenny. Second, by havin' it seem that you killed her, Duke made sure a lot of men in this town'd be real sore at you."

"That was pretty clever," Jim admitted.

"I'll tell Duke you said so. He'll appreciate that." Castle answered. "Now, move out. Who knows? Mebbe you'll get lucky, Ranger, and I'll miss you. You really might get away," he said, with a vicious laugh.

"All right."

Jim walked slowly toward the cell door. Castle stood aside to let him pass, his gun now aimed at the Ranger's stomach, the hammer thumbed back. When Jim was abreast of the marshal, he paused, pulled the knife from behind his back, and lunged at Castle, grabbing for his gun.

Castle dropped the gun's hammer just as Jim attempted to twist it from his grasp. Jim wedged the web of skin between his thumb and forefinger under the hammer, wincing with pain, but preventing it from striking the cartridge and sending a bullet into him. He slashed at the marshal's forearm, the knife's blade slicing through tendon and muscle. Blood spurted, splattering over Jim's shirtfront. His arm paralyzed with pain, Castle lost his grip on the gun. It clattered to the floor, ripping Jim's skin. Jim then plunged his knife into Castle's belly, driving it deep and thrusting upward, tearing through intestines and puncturing the marshal's stomach. Castle gasped, his eyes wide with shock. He folded, blood gushing from his ripped-open abdomen. Jim shoved him back, pulling the knife from his middle, then slashed the marshal's throat to prevent him from screaming. Castle slumped to the floor. Stepping over the dying marshal, Jim slid the knife behind his shirt, picked up Castle's gun, and shoved it behind his own belt.

Jim hurried to the front office, where he found his own Peacemaker and gunbelt in a bottom desk drawer, along with his Bowie. The gunbelt he buckled around his waist, then shoved the knife into the sheath on his belt. There were two boxes of cartridges in that same drawer. Jim pocketed these. That done, he located his Winchester, which was in the gun rack along with Castle's saddle guns. Jim yanked the rifle from the shelf and sprinted out the front door.

As much as he wanted Sizzle, his big paint, beneath him for his flight, Jim realized he had only a slim chance of making it past the several saloons, including the Quicksilver and Panhandle Palace, which were still open at this hour, and which stood between him and the Horse Heaven Livery. There were always a few men gathered on the boardwalks in front of those establishments. Instead of trying for the stable, Jim chose a blocky bay, which was hitched just down the street from the jail. The gelding appeared to have both speed and bottom.

"Easy, boy," he soothed the horse, which snorted at his approach. He untied the bay's reins, climbed into the saddle, and eased him away from the rail. Jim pulled his hat low, then walked the bay slowly down the street, hoping to avoid being recognized.

Luck was with him. The streets were virtually empty, most citizens of Quitaque having long since retired, while the denizens of the saloons and gambling halls were mainly inside, occupied with their drinking, gambling, and women. The bay's owner was evidently among them, for no hue and cry was raised about the horse being stolen. The Ranger reached the edge of town unmolested.

Once Jim passed the last structure on Main Street, he put the bay into a dead run. He needed to reach the sheltering canyons and draws of the Caprock before sunup.

Chapter Seven

Duffy McGlynn stumbled out of the Quicksilver, half-fell down the stairs, then weaved his way up the street. To celebrate his eighteenth birthday, the young cowpuncher had been granted an extra day off from his job at the Circle G Ranch. He'd taken full advantage of the opportunity in grand style, starting at the Panhandle Palace, finishing up at the Quicksilver, and stopping at every saloon along the way. In between, he'd spent some time with a couple of the ladies at Molly's, who were more than willing to help the big, blonde, good-looking cowboy lose his virginity to commemorate his milestone birth date. Now Duffy, reeling from the effects of all that liquor, staggered his way to where he thought he'd left his horse. He stopped, staring blankly at the empty space where he remembered tying his bay. McGlynn thumbed back his Stetson and scratched his head.

"Cactus? Now where'd he go? I could'a sworn I tied him right here."

McGlynn walked down two more blocks, searching in vain for his gelding. Not finding him, he returned to where he was positive he'd left the horse.

"Cactus?" he repeated. "Where'd you run off to? You'd better not have headed back to the ranch without me, blast you, horse. If I have to walk home, you..."

He cut loose with a string of oaths, concluding with some very disparaging comments about Cactus' breeding and ancestry.

A second floor window over the dry goods store slid open, and the shop's sleepy-eyed owner peered out.

"Hey, you. What's all that commotion down there?" he demanded of McGlynn. "Don't you realize what time it is? It's the middle of the night. Decent folks are tryin' to get some sleep. I don't mind you cowpokes raisin' a ruckus on Friday or Saturday nights, but not during the week. You quiet down or I'll send for the marshal."

"I'm sorry, Mister," McGlynn answered. "I'm looking for my horse. I'm certain I left him right here in front of your store, but I can't find neither hide nor hair of him."

"Your horse? Was he a chunky bay gelding, with a wide blaze on his face?" the storekeeper questioned.

"Yeah. That's him. His name's Cactus," McGlynn confirmed.

"I saw an hombre take that horse about an hour ago," the shopkeeper stated. "Didn't pay no mind to him, since I figured it was his cayuse. I'm afraid your horse has been stolen, son. You'd better find the marshal and report it."

"Cactus? Stolen?" Duffy repeated, not quite sure of what he'd heard.

"That's what I said," the shopkeeper reiterated. "Whoever took him didn't act like he was in any hurry. He headed north, keeping that horse to a walk."

"Thanks. Thanks, Mister," McGlynn stammered. He turned on his heels, pausing for a moment as his head spun, then started for the marshal's office. He attempted to run, but merely managed a stumbling, shuffling fast walk.

McGlynn reached the office a few minutes later. He climbed the stairs and pushed open the door.

"Marshal! Marshal Castle! You here? My horse was stolen."

McGlynn's shouts were answered with silence.

"Marshal?" he called again, more softly. "It's Duffy. Duffy McGlynn. Where are you, Marshal?"

When McGlynn's eyes became accustomed to the gloomy interior of the office, he noticed the door separating the cells from the office was half-ajar.

"Marshal? You back there, bunkin' in one of the cells?" he questioned.

McGlynn stepped through the door, then recoiled, his guts churning at the sight of the bloody corpse of Marshal Castle. Castle was lying face-up, his right forearm deeply slashed, his throat slit, and his belly sliced open from belt almost to breastbone. The marshal's unseeing eyes were wide open with the shock and horror of his sudden demise. Blood pooled around his body.

Gagging and retching, McGlynn turned and ran for air. He lurched out of the office, stumbled, fell, and rolled down the stairs. He came to his hands and knees in the dusty street. The cowboy vomited violently, his stomach losing every drop of liquor he'd consumed that night.

McGlynn finally regained some semblance of control. Shuddering, he pulled his pistol from its holster. He managed to pull himself upright, and fired three shots into the air.

"Murder!" he screamed. "The Marshal's been killed! Somebody get some help!"

McGlynn fired the remaining two bullets in the gun.

"There's been a killin'!" he again shouted.

Men poured from the saloons, heading for where McGlynn stood in the middle of the road, still calling for help.

Duke Ballantine pushed his way through the mob, with Joe Hardy at his side. Right behind them was John Baker.

"What's that you're sayin', cowboy?" Ballantine demanded.

"The marshal," McGlynn shakily replied. He pointed at the office. "He's lyin' in there, dead as a doornail. Somebody sliced his brisket wide open."

"The Ranger!" Ballantine exploded. He grabbed McGlynn's shoulders.

"Was there anyone in the cells?" he shouted at the

flustered cowboy.

"I dunno," McGlynn answered.

Ballantine shook McGlynn fiercely.

"Think, you drunken idiot. Was there anyone in the cells?"

"I told you, I dunno," McGlynn repeated, now shocked almost fully sober. "I didn't take the time to look. I just wanted to get outta there as fast as I could."

Ballantine shoved McGlynn aside.

"Joe, you come with me." He chose two others. "Whiskey, Dude, you also. The rest of you stay here."

"I'm comin' too," John Baker insisted.

"All right," Ballantine agreed. "I reckon you'd better."

Ballantine and Baker took the lead as the five men went inside the office, while the rest crowded around the front door.

Baker was the first to spot the marshal's body.

"There's Castle," he said.

"And Blawcyzk's cell is wide open," Ballantine answered, with a curse. "I told Castle to be careful with him."

"Someone must've smuggled that Ranger a knife, or else he found something sharp in his cell," Whiskey Shannon observed.

"It had to be real sharp, to rip open Castle's gut like that," Hardy answered.

"That doesn't matter now. What does matter is getting on Blawcyzk's trail before he gets too much of a start," Baker said.

"What's that, John? You're finally convinced Blawcyzk's nothing more than a lousy killer?" Ballantine asked.

"I'll have to admit it," Baker conceded. "It looks like you were right all along, Duke."

"We're wastin' time standin' around here," Dude Bannon pointed out. "We should be askin' that cowboy how he happened by the marshal's office."

"You're right," Ballantine agreed. "Let's just hope he's sobered up enough to remember why."

The group tramped outside, where they had to force their way through the mob surrounding the front door. By now the crowd had grown larger, as townsfolk roused from their sleep rushed to see what had caused such a commotion. Shouted questions rose on the still night air.

"What happened?" "Is the marshal really dead?" "Who killed him?" "Did the Ranger escape?"

"Quiet, all of you," Ballantine ordered. He called McGlynn. "Duffy, come over here."

"All right." McGlynn shuffled to where Ballantine, Baker, and the others stood.

"Duffy, why'd you stop at the marshal's office?" Ballantine asked.

"My horse, Cactus, was stolen," McGlynn answered.

"I couldn't find him when I went lookin' for him. At first I thought he'd run off, but the hombre who owns the dry goods store said he'd been stolen. He saw somebody ride away on him. So, I went to tell Marshal Castle that someone'd stolen my horse. That's when I found the marshal, lyin' dead with his belly sliced open like you'd gut a steer."

A murmur swept through the bystanders.

"Stay quiet until we're done," Baker ordered. "You said Sol Grossman saw whoever stole your horse, Duffy?"

"That's right," McGlynn answered.

"Did Sol get a look at him?" Baker continued.

"Nope. He claimed the horse thief rode off at a walk, like he wasn't worried at all, so he figured that Cactus belonged to whoever took him."

"That had to be the Ranger!" Hardy exclaimed.

"It would seem so," Ballantine agreed. "Duffy, did Sol say about when your horse was taken?'

"Let's see," McGlynn thought. "He said about an hour ago. Then it took me a few minutes to reach the marshal's office, and a couple more to get my senses back after I found Marshal Castle. I'd reckon Cactus was stolen anywhere from an hour to an hour and a half ago. Two hours at the most."

"That means Blawcyzk already has a good start," Hardy observed. He glanced at the moonless sky, where scudding mare's tail clouds obscured much of the dim starlight.

"It's a new moon, so it'll be pitch black outside of town," Hardy continued. "We won't be able to trail Blawcyzk tonight. We'll have to wait until sunup. How many of you will be ready to ride at first light?"

Most of the men raised their hands as they muttered an assent.

"Hold on just a minute," Baker objected. "With Castle dead we need to appoint a new marshal, at least temporarily."

"John's right," Ike Waters agreed. "I say give Joe Hardy the job."

"I'm for that," Ballantine said. "How about the rest of you?"

A chorus of "yeas" went up.

"Not so fast," Baker protested.

"What's wrong, John? You don't want Hardy as marshal?" Ballantine challenged.

"He wouldn't be my choice, no," Baker confirmed. "Although at this moment, he's the only man who even comes halfway near bein' qualified. However, we want to make sure we do things legally, especially since we're talkin' about hunting down a Texas Ranger. A man who, I might add, probably won't surrender. That means killin' him. When Ranger Headquarters questions what happened, we want to make sure we've crossed all our t's and dotted all our i's."

"What're you sayin', John?" Chauncey Brennan asked. The hostler had been awakened by McGlynn's gunshots, and had hurried from his stable.

"We need to have a quorum of the town council appoint Hardy marshal," Baker explained. "That means at least five members. I'm on the council, and so are you, Chauncey. Ike Waters, you are also. Tom Doyle's here. He's the chairman. We need one more member."

"What about Sol Grossman?" Ballantine suggested. "We need to talk with him anyway, to see if he can give us more information. Since he saw the hombre who stole Duffy's horse, mebbe he can confirm who it was... not that there's any doubt of that. So let's go get Grossman. He can answer our questions, then, with his vote, the council can legally appoint Hardy marshal."

"All right," Baker agreed. "Let's wake Sol up."

The group headed down to Grossman's. The dry goods store owner had gone back to sleep after speaking with McGlynn, and had somehow slept through the ensuing commotion.

Ballantine rapped sharply on the front door.

"Sol. Wake up!" he called, knocking again.

A second floor window opened, and Grossman poked his head out.

"What is it now? Can't a man get any sleep in this town?" he querulously shouted.

"We're sorry, Sol," Baker responded. "But Marshal Castle's been murdered. Apparently Jim Blawcyzk somehow broke jail, killed Castle, and escaped. We need to hold an emergency town council meeting right now, so we can appoint

Joe Hardy temporary marshal. That way he can form a posse and start on the Ranger's trail as soon as it's daylight."

"I'll be right down," Grossman answered. "Just give me a minute to get dressed."

He ducked back inside. When he did, his wife's voice drifted to the men below.

"Sol, what's happening?"

"The marshal's been killed, Sophie. I have to go," Grossman answered.

"I'm coming with you," his wife replied.

"Then get dressed, quickly," he ordered.

A few moments later, Grossman and his wife joined the crowd gathered around the store.

"All right, let's call this meeting," he said. "Mebbe then I can at least get a little sleep."

"Not quite so fast, Sol," Ballantine answered. "Duffy McGlynn says you saw whoever stole his horse."

"That's right," Grossman confirmed.

"Was it the Ranger?"

"I don't know," Grossman replied. "It's too dark to see a man plainly once the sun sets. That's why, for months, I've been askin' the rest of the council to approve street lamps. I've seen those in other towns. The marshal usually is the man who lights them, as he makes his rounds. However, no one wants to spend the money for 'em. Mebbe now that it's too late you'll finally see things my way."

Bullet for a Ranger

"Sol, forget that for now," Baker said. "All right. You can't say for sure it was Blawcyzk who stole Duffy's horse. Can you at least tell us which way the man headed?"

"Sure. Like I told that cowboy, he headed north. I'd imagine he'll aim for the Caprock. He probably figures on losin' himself there. I wish I'd known that hombre was a horse thief. I'd have blasted him with my shotgun."

"It's a good thing you didn't try that, Sol," Ballantine stated. "Blawcyzk's a cold-blooded killer. Even with a Greener, you wouldn't have stood a chance against him."

"Duke's right, Sol," Sophie agreed. "And I'm not ready to be a widow. Not quite yet."

"Let's finish our business," Chauncey Brennan suggested. "That way we can take care of Marshal Castle's remains, and the possemen will be able to grab a couple hours of sleep."

"Fine," Baker said. "Tom, call the council to order."

Tom Doyle, the bartender from the Quicksilver, climbed onto the porch in front of Grossman's. Once Baker, Brennan, Waters, and Grossman joined him, Doyle called the meeting.

"There's only one order of business," he stated, "which is the appointment of Joe Hardy as temporary town marshal of Quitaque. The appointment will authorize Joe to deputize as many men as he sees fit, in order to recapture Jim Blawcyzk."

"There is one technicality," Ike Waters, the hardware store owner and undertaker, pointed out. "Joe's authority won't extend beyond the town limits."

"Don't worry about that," Hardy assured him. "Once we catch up to that Ranger, we'll make sure and kill him. Then we'll either leave him for the buzzards and coyotes, or bring his body back here and say he was killed in town. Even that's more'n he deserves."

"That solves that," Ballantine called out.

"All right. I move that Joe Hardy be appointed town marshal," Sol Grossman said.

"I second," said Ike Waters.

"All in favor?" Doyle asked.

"Aye."

"It's unanimous. Joe, raise your right hand."

Hardy was sworn in as Walt Castle's replacement.

"Joe, you now have the authority to deputize a posse," Doyle concluded, once the oath was administered.

"Fine. Any of you men who want to ride with me, meet me in front of Brennan's livery a half-hour before sunup," Duffy ordered. "Right now, I'd like a couple of you to help me get Walt Castle's body to Ike's place."

"I'll give you a hand," Dude Bannon offered. John Baker and Chauncey Brennan also volunteered, as did Waters, the undertaker himself.

While some of the men and women drifted home, most, morbidly curious, followed Hardy and the others to the marshal's office and jail. They waited outside until Castle's body was removed, then followed along as the marshal's remains were carried to Water's Hardware and Mortuary. Castle was taken to a back room, laid on a wooden bench, and covered with a canvas tarp.

"I guess that's all we can do for Walt until morning," Waters stated. "It's gonna be a hot day, so we'll need to have his service right quick."

"That'll be up to you, Ike," Hardy said. "Most of us'll be on the trail of Walt's killer."

"All right, I'll see to the arrangements," Waters answered.

"You can bill the town," Baker told him.

"Thanks," Waters answered. "Now if you don't mind, I'm headed back to bed."

"That's a smart idea, for all of us," Ballantine answered. "Good night, Ike."

"'Night, Duke. 'Night, all of you."

* * *

While the rest of Quitaque headed home, Ballantine, Foley, and the rest of Ballantine's men went back to the Quicksilver. Tom Doyle was not with them, Ballantine making sure to send his chief bartender home.

The Quicksilver's owner opened a bottle of whiskey, placed several glasses on the bar, and filled them.

"Blast that Castle," Ballantine said, once everyone had had a drink. "Joe, didn't I tell him to wait until you and a couple of your men were with him before turnin' that Ranger loose?"

"You sure did," Hardy confirmed.

"But he didn't listen, did he? He had to try'n be the hero on his own, and what'd it get him? A knife in the guts, and now Blawcyzk's roamin' free. That's the last thing we needed."

"I wouldn't worry too much about that, Duke," Hardy advised. "That Ranger wouldn't dare turn up, not if he has any brains. He's probably holed up somewhere in the Caprock, figurin' to lay low for a few days, then make a break for the Territories. We'll find him. And when we do, he won't get away again. We'll fill him so full of lead he'd break a horse's back."

"See that you do," Ballantine grumbled.

"Speaking of that knife he stuck in Castle's belly, I wonder how Blawcyzk got his hands on it," Mike Putney said.

"I dunno. Who's been visitin' him?" Ballantine asked.

"John Baker, but he hadn't been by the jail for several days," Hardy answered. "The only other visitor Blawcyzk had was that priest, Campos."

"You think a priest might have smuggled that knife to Blawcyzk?" Dude Bannon questioned.

"It sounds far-fetched, but who else could have?" Hardy mused.

"No one," Ballantine replied. "Joe, I reckon before you try huntin' down Blawcyzk, you'll have to have a talk with that Bible thumper. He probably knows where the Ranger headed. I'm certain you can convince Campos to reveal what he knows."

"It'll be a pleasure," Hardy grinned. "In fact, let's go visit him right now."

* * *

Joe Hardy and the posse spent two days combing the Caprock. They had followed the tracks of Jim's stolen horse to within five miles of the rugged escarpment, then Jim had turned off the main trail. Once the Ranger entered the labyrinth of canyons lacing the Caprock, his horse's tracks soon disappeared on the flinty soil.

The Caprock is the dividing line between the High Plains and the lower lands to the south and east. North and west of the Caprock lies the Llano Estacado, or Staked Plains, the flat and virtually featureless tableland which extends for hundreds of miles. Spanish padres bringing the Faith to the New World had been forced to place stakes along their routes, to avoid becoming hopelessly lost. South and east are the more fertile, moister plains of central and east Texas. The Caprock even has some effect on climate. Moisture from the Gulf of Mexico often becomes trapped below the escarpment, keeping the land to the north and west dryer, less suited to farming than ranching.

The Caprock itself is a rugged maze of canyons,

draws, and breaks, stretching for miles. It's an ideal place for a man wanting to get away by himself for a time... or for a man on the run from the law. It was here that Jim Blawcyzk had disappeared. With his years of experience trailing outlaws throughout the length and breadth of Texas, and his knowledge of the dimmest back trails, it would be next to impossible for most men to find him. After those two fruitless days of searching for the Ranger, Hardy and the posse had returned to Quitaque to rest, resupply, and obtain fresh horses.

Following a night's rest, they had gathered in front of Brennan's Horse Heaven. It was just about an hour past sunrise. The men were readying their mounts, preparing for several more days of looking for Jim. Besides Hardy and his posse, several others were with them, including John Baker and Duke Ballantine. It was Ballantine who first spotted an approaching horseman.

"Someone's comin'," he said.

"You don't reckon that Ranger'd be fool enough to come back?" Mike Putney asked.

"I can't tell who it is, but it's not Blawcyzk," Ballantine answered. "He's not that stupid."

The men watched as the approaching rider drew nearer. He was dressed almost completely in black, except for a bright red bandanna around his neck. His horse was a steeldust, the dark gray complementing his rider's outfit. Unlike most men, this one wore two guns, in black holsters hanging from the finely tooled black leather gunbelt encircling his slim waist. Finally, the rider came close enough so the silver star on silver circle badge glittering on his vest could be seen. Now, as he approached, his features became clearer. The rider was slightly smaller than average in height, but with a wiry build. His black Stetson covered most of his hair, but what showed under the hat was black, frosted at the tips. It gave the illusion of a puff of smoke. He had a pencil-thin mustache, somewhat shadowed by the several days worth of dark whiskers covering his jaw. His dark eyes held an inscrutability in their depths as he narrowly studied the posse.

The newcomer touched the brim of his Stetson. He searched out the evident leader of the group, Joe Hardy, who now wore a marshal's badge. His gaze locked on Hardy.

"Mornin', gents," he said. "I'm Texas Ranger Smoky McCue. Marshal, I understand you've got my pardner, Jim Blawcyzk, locked up. I want to see him right now."

"We did have him in jail, Ranger," Hardy answered. "But he's gone. Escaped. He broke out, gutted Walt Castle, the previous marshal, stole a horse, and took off. Near as we can tell, he's holed up somewhere in the Caprock. Either that or he's long gone and is across the Red, someplace in the Territories. We've been scourin' the Caprock for two days, tryin' to find him. We came back for more supplies and fresh broncs. We're about ready to take his trail again. You want to come with us?"

"Just wait a minute, Marshal," Smoky ordered. "First off, you haven't bothered to give me your name."

"It's Hardy. Joe Hardy."

"Fine. Marshal Hardy, I understand there are some pretty serious charges against Jim. I'd like to hear a little more about those before I do anything," Smoky requested.

"Let me handle this, Joe," Ballantine spoke up. "Ranger, I'm Duke Ballantine, owner of the Quicksilver Saloon. Your partner, Lieutenant Blawcyzk, got liquored up, took Jenny Cole, one of my girls, upstairs, had an argument with her, and stabbed her to death. I heard the fight, and found Blawcyzk passed out in Jenny's bed. Her body was alongside him, with his knife stuck in her chest."

"That doesn't sound at all like Jim," Smoky protested. "I've never seen him take a drink of anything stronger than sarsaparilla. As far as him goin' to bed with a saloon gal, that's ridiculous. Jim'd never cheat on his wife. In fact, he'd barely look at another woman."

An enigmatic grin crossed Smoky's countenance for just a moment, as he briefly remembered one lady who did capture Jim's attention, a spectacularly beautiful flamenco dancer named Therese Marchitto. He and Jim had made the acquaintance of that woman some time back, in the east-central Texas town of Bartlett, when they were on the trail of a band of outlaws who'd shot Jim and his son Charlie, assaulted and raped Jim's wife Julia, and left them all for dead.[1]

"Mebbeso, but there are plenty of witnesses who saw him go to Jenny's room," Ballantine replied. "And there's absolutely no doubt he killed Marshal Castle. None whatsoever."

[1] *The story of the attack on Jim's family and his search for the men responsible is told in* Ranger's Revenge, *from Silverjack Publishing.*

John Baker came forward.

"I'm afraid Duke is right, Ranger," he said. "I'm John Baker, the man who originally asked for assistance from Austin. I had hoped your partner would get to the bottom of the trouble here in Quitaque. When he was accused of murder, I believed him when he said he was innocent, and that he'd been framed. I'm the one who sent his request for help to Austin. Clearly, I was mistaken. His knifing the marshal and escaping proves that."

"It proves nothing, except mebbe Jim felt he had no choice," Smoky snapped. His voice grew quieter, but somehow more menacing. "It seems like y'all are awfully anxious to hang him for a crime he probably didn't commit."

Another man detached himself from the assemblage. His hair and beard were gray, and his eyes, also gray, were hidden by a pair of thick spectacles. He wore a dark, ill-fitting suit and string tie.

"See here, Ranger," he said. "I'm Circuit Judge Reilly Tucker. I arrived here in Quitaque to preside over Ranger Blawcyzk's trial, only to find that he had killed Marshal Castle and broken jail. It is your sworn duty as an officer of the State of Texas to do everything in your power to apprehend Ranger Blawcyzk, who is now a fugitive from the law."

"You mean allegedly killed the marshal," Smoky retorted. "Jim hasn't been tried and convicted yet, Judge. I shouldn't have to remind you a man is presumed innocent until found guilty. As far as my pardner goes, I have every intention of findin' him," Smoky answered. "But I'm not gonna be part of a lynch mob, men hidin' behind deputy's badges, tryin' to make everything appear nice and legal. I'll bring Jim in, but on my own terms."

"We have no intention of letting you go after Blawcyzk on your own, Ranger," Hardy objected. "How do we know you wouldn't just help him get clean away?"

"Because this badge means I'm sworn to uphold the law, and I'll do just that," Smoky snarled. "If some of you want to ride with me, that's fine, but I'm not lettin' the whole bunch of you join me. And let me make this clear. Once we do catch up to Jim, I'll handle him. I don't need to remind you, Marshal, your jurisdiction ends at the town limits."

"I believe those terms are acceptable," Ballantine said. "Aren't they, Marshal?"

"I reckon," was Hardy's surly reply.

"All right. Now we understand each other," Smoky said. "I've been ridin' hard, and spent the last few nights sleepin' on the rocky ground. My horse needs a good feedin' and rest, and so do I. I'll be ready to head out in three hours."

"But that'll give Blawcyzk even more time to put distance behind him," Ballantine complained.

Smoky eyed Sizzle and Sam, who were pacing restlessly in one of the livery's corrals.

"Those are Jim's horses back there. He wouldn't go far without them," Smoky explained. "He's just bidin' his time until he can come back for them."

"A man facin' a noose sure ain't gonna worry about a couple of broncs," Ike Waters disagreed.

"You don't know Jim," Smoky replied. "He'd rather die'n leave his horses behind. Now, that's enough talk. Where can I grab a bit of shut-eye? And like I mentioned, ol' Soot here needs feedin', waterin', and a good rubdown."

Chauncey Brennan stepped forward.

"I'll handle your horse, Ranger," he offered. "I've been caring for Ranger Blawcyzk's mounts since he arrived."

Smoky eyed the duded-up man with the English accent and top hat dubiously.

"Even Sam?" he questioned.

"Even Samuel," Brennan affirmed. "He seems to have taken a liking to me."

"Then if you can handle that ornery cayuse, I'm certain you'll take good care of Soot," Smoky answered. He dismounted and handed the steeldust's reins to Brennan.

"I've got a couple of empty rooms in my hotel, Ranger McCue. You're welcome to one of them," Baker offered.

"That's fine," Smoky replied, "And thanks."

"Perhaps you'd like to examine the room where Jenny Cole was killed before you rest," Ballantine suggested.

"There's no need for that," Smoky replied. "I'm sure your late marshal collected all the evidence it contained. After we catch up with Jim, I'll have plenty of time to look it over." He left unsaid the obvious fact that the room had no doubt long since been swept clean by the real killer and whoever he worked for.

"Then if you're ready, my hotel's right down the street," Baker said.

"All right," Smoky replied. He turned to Joe Hardy.

"Marshal, pick out three or four men to ride with us. Meet me back here in three hours."

"Okay," Hardy agreed. "Anythin' else, Ranger?"

"Not right now. However, it'd be helpful if you had some idea which way Jim went. That'd narrow our search some," Smoky explained.

"I don't, and we sure haven't had much luck finding any sign of him," Hardy said. "The Caprock's plumb riddled with canyons and ravines. In some of those places, you could ride within five feet of a man and never even know he was there."

"There is one person who we think might know where Blawcyzk headed, but he won't talk," Baker added.

"Who's that?" Smoky asked.

"The priest from the Catholic mission, Father Campos," Baker answered.

"The padre smuggled a knife to Blawcyzk. That's how he was able to kill Marshal Castle and break jail," Hardy stated.

"A priest?" Smoky said, "That seems pretty unlikely."

"I know, but he's the only one who visited the Ranger the last few days. No one else could have gotten a weapon into his cell. The priest must've hidden the knife under his robes," Hardy responded. "We've had Campos locked up, but he's kept his mouth shut."

"Even when Marshal Hardy explained to the padre he could be charged as an accessory to murder, and also face hanging," Ballantine concluded.

"The only thing you have against the priest is that he visited Jim?" Smoky said. "That's hardly enough evidence to even arrest him, let alone hold him for trial. I need to talk to him."

"Of course," Hardy agreed. "Mebbe you can get somethin' out of him. The jail's across the street from Baker's hotel, so it's on the way."

"Then let's go, Marshal."

* * *

When they reached the marshal's office, Smoky stopped at the foot of the steps.

"I want to speak with the padre alone," he said. "He might give me some information he wouldn't reveal with anyone else listenin'. Marshal, you and I'll go inside. You'll let me in the cell, then wait out here. I'll call when I'm ready to leave."

"I can't let you do that, Ranger," Hardy protested. "I

can just as easily wait in the front office."

"You'll wait out here, Marshal. I don't want any eavesdroppin'. Do I make myself clear?" Smoky retorted. "And don't even think of standin' outside the cell window, either. I'll check."

"Ranger McCue is right, Joe," Ballantine broke in. "Let him have that private talk with the priest. Perhaps he will find out something, if Campos lets his guard down."

"All right," Hardy conceded. "But I still don't like the idea."

"I don't much care what you like or don't like," Smoky snapped. "Now let me in that cell."

Reluctantly, Hardy led Smoky into his office. He lifted a ring of keys from a peg, opened the oak door leading to the cells, and stepped inside the corridor.

"I've got a visitor for you, priest," he grumbled. "A Ranger. He's got some questions for you. Mebbe you'll finally realize the mistake you've made, and tell him where Blawczyk is hidin'."

Smoky and Father Campos waited silently while Hardy unlocked the cell and admitted the Ranger. Once Hardy had departed, closing the heavy oak door behind him, Smoky introduced himself.

"Father, I'm Smoky McCue. Cap'n Trumbull sent me up here from Austin, after he got a message from Jim Blawcyzk sayin' he'd been arrested for murder. It appears Jim's in quite a bit of trouble."

"I'm certainly glad to see you, Ranger McCue. I'm

Father Miguel Campos. Jim had hoped you would be the man Captain Trumbull sent. I'm afraid your partner is in deep trouble," Father Campos said.

Smoky studied the padre for a moment. Father Campos had the typical appearance of a Spanish-ancestry Texan or Mexican, a dark complexion, thick black hair, and dark brown eyes. To Smoky, those eyes seemed particularly kind. Anger boiled up within the Ranger at the sight of the bruises marring Father Campos' face and his split open lower lip.

"Did the marshal and his men do that to you, Father?" he asked.

"They did," the priest confirmed. "They wanted to make me reveal where Jim might be hiding. I didn't, of course."

"Father, Marshal Hardy claims you smuggled a knife to Jim, and that's what enabled him to escape," Smoky continued. "What do you have to say about that?"

"As I told the marshal, the very notion of a priest giving a weapon to an accused murderer is preposterous," Father Campos replied.

"That doesn't really answer the question, does it?"

Smoky couldn't help but chuckle.

"No, I guess it doesn't," the priest admitted.

"So, did you give Jim a knife?"

"I'll let you draw your own conclusion, Ranger," Father Campos answered.

Again, Smoky had to chuckle.

"All right. And please, Father, call me Smoky."

"Certainly."

"Thanks. Father, I have to ask this. What did you and Jim discuss during your visits?"

"I can't reveal much," Father Campos explained. "We talked about his family, of course. He wanted to make sure, if anything did happen to him, they knew he loved them. He also wanted to let them know he hadn't done anything to make them ashamed of him."

"You must have talked about Jim's bein' accused of murder," Smoky said.

"Naturally. And of course I heard Jim's Confession, and gave him Holy Eucharist," Father Campos answered. "I can't discuss anything Jim may have revealed during his Confession. I trust you understand that, unlike Marshal Hardy."

"I do," Smoky answered. "I learned about that from Jim. However, you must be convinced that Jim is innocent."

"All I can say is that he confessed his sins to me," Father Campos reiterated. "You can imply what you wish."

"What I'm guessin' is that Jim didn't confess to killin' that girl, or you wouldn't have helped him escape. Is that right, Father?" Smoky pressed.

"I can't say more than I already have," the priest insisted.

"I understand," Smoky replied.

"Thank you."

"Father, the marshal seems to think you have an idea where Jim headed. Is he right?" Smoky questioned.

"Only a vague one," Father Campos admitted. "Of course, he was hoping to avoid having to take flight at all. Failing that, he hoped you or another Ranger would show up. He said, if one did, for me to let him know Jim would be waiting somewhere in the Caprock, about eight or ten miles northeast of here. He also said he'd leave sign that most men wouldn't spot, but which a Ranger should be able to follow without too much trouble. He planned on waiting for two weeks. After that, if help hadn't arrived, he would head into the Indian Territories."

"You mean Jim reckoned on fleeing Texas?" Smoky exclaimed.

"Do you really believe that, Smoky?" Father Campos asked.

"No."

"Neither do I. I'm sure that information was meant as a diversion, just in case I did reveal it."

"Or he was protectin' you, Father. Mebbe he wanted you to let that slip, figurin' once the marshal had what he wanted, he'd leave you be," Smoky pointed out.

"Perhaps," the priest agreed. "So what now?"

"I'm gonna find Jim," Smoky answered. "Hardy

and a few men are ridin' with me. I can't stop 'em, but I can make, uh, dang sure they won't shoot him on sight, or lynch him."

Father Campos smiled as Smoky stumbled when he nearly cursed.

"Then I'll pray for you and Jim. I'll also give you the Lord's blessing."

"I'm not Catholic. I'm Methodist," Smoky objected.

"I don't think our Lord makes that distinction," the priest grinned.

"I guess you're right, Father," Smoky conceded. He removed his hat and bowed his head while Father Campos made the Sign of the Cross over him.

"*In nomine Patris, et Filii, et Spiritus Sancti. Amen.*"

"Thanks, Father," Smoky said. "Now, I reckon I'd best be on my way. I'm gonna take a couple hours shut-eye, then start on Jim's trail."

Smoky raised his voice to call Joe Hardy.

"Marshal! I'm ready."

A moment later, the marshal reappeared.

"Did this hombre tell you anythin', Ranger?" he demanded, before unlocking the cell door.

"He's not an hombre, he's a man of God, and you'd better give him the respect he deserves," Smoky retorted. "Now open this cell."

"All right."

Hardy turned the key and unlocked the door. Smoky emerged from the cell, then turned and beckoned to Father Campos.

"All right, Father. You've spent enough time behind bars," he said. "You're free to go."

"What do you think you're doin', Ranger?" Hardy protested. "This man's a prisoner. He aided a jail break."

"You've got absolutely no proof of that, and no reason to hold him," Smoky answered. "Now let him go, before I toss you in that cell for false arrest, Marshal."

"As long as you're takin' the responsibility, Ranger," Hardy said.

"I am."

"Fine."

"Thanks, Smoky," Father Campos said. He stepped out of the cell.

When the trio emerged from the jail, there was a murmur of protest at the sight of the priest.

"What's the priest doin' out of his cell, Ranger?" Ballantine demanded. "He helped Blawcyzk escape."

"There's no evidence of that whatsoever," Smoky answered. "I'm turnin' Father Campos loose, and if I hear of anyone harassin' him, that man'll have to answer to me."

Smoky spun and punched Joe Hardy solidly on the jaw. The blow knocked the marshal flat on his back.

"That's for hittin' a priest, Marshal," Smoky growled.

"Anyone else want more of the same?"

Smoky's challenge was answered by dead silence.

"I didn't think so," he said. "Now get out of here, all of you."

"Smoky, you shouldn't have done that," Father Campos scolded. The grin on his face belied his objection. Under his breath, he added, "But I have to admit, I enjoyed it. May God be with you. Vaya con Dios."

Chapter Eight

AFTER SUCCESSFULLY making his getaway, Jim pulled the bay to a walk about two miles out of town. He walked the horse for a mile, stopped to allow the animal a short breather, then put him into a steady jog. Jim's practiced eye for horseflesh hadn't failed him. The bay had exceptionally smooth gaits, and seemed willing to travel at that slow trot indefinitely. Jim kept him at that pace for another three miles, then slowed him to a walk once again. He held the horse to the walk for two miles, then pushed him into a lope. The first glimpses of the jagged cliffs and rugged canyons of the Caprock were coming into view. Soon they would begin pressing in on the trail.

With the first gray light of the false dawn streaking the eastern horizon, Jim chose the first canyon he came to. He turned the tiring gelding left into its maw, letting the horse pick his own way. After a mile of winding through the brush, the bay pricked up his ears and broke into a trot when he scented water. Soon a small patch of greenery appeared. In its center was a small pool of clear water. A small creek trickled from the pool, disappearing behind a maze of shattered boulders.

The horse nickered eagerly and strained at his reins.

"Easy, boy," Jim told the bay. "Wouldn't do for you to drink too much water too fast and make yourself sick. We're gonna rest here until nightfall, so you'll have plenty of time to drink and graze."

Jim let the horse reach the edge of the pool before reining him to a stop and dismounting. He let the animal have a short drink, then pulled him back.

"You can have some more in a little bit," Jim promised. "Once I get you unsaddled and rubbed down."

Jim removed saddle and bridle from the bay, slipping a rope halter he found in the saddlebags over the gelding's head. When he dropped the saddle to the ground, he noticed the word "Cactus" engraved in the breastplate.

"Huh. Cactus," Jim muttered. "Reckon that must be your name, fella," he said to the bay. The gelding pricked up his ears in recognition. "Well, Cactus, I reckon it's time to take care of you," Jim continued. "And with luck, I'll have you reunited with your owner in a short while."

He tied the horse to a juniper, leaving enough slack so the gelding could crop at the sparse grass. While Cactus grazed, Jim took a worn currycomb from the saddlebags and used it to comb dirt and sweat from the bay's hide. Once he was finished, he let the horse drink his fill, then picketed him to roll and graze.

"You just relax, fella," Jim told Cactus, with a rub of the horse's velvety muzzle. "We're gonna be puttin' some miles behind us again tonight, so I need you well-rested."

The first rays of the rising sun were now penetrating into the canyon. With the horse cared for, Jim turned his attention to himself. The hammer of Castle's gun had torn a deep gash in the web of skin between Jim's thumb and forefinger. That gash throbbed with pain. Jim emptied the saddlebags, looking in vain for any medicinal salves. Finding none, he soaked the gash in the waterhole for a few moments. After that, he emptied the contents of the saddlebags. Some packages of jerky spilled out, along with another box of cartridges.

"That's one break, anyway," Jim muttered. "I've got some extra bullets, and more importantly a little food. It wouldn't do to try'n shoot any game for supper, not yet. Mebbe in a couple of days."

Jim ate several strips of the tough, stringy meat, washing it down with water from the pool. His hunger partially sated, Jim pulled off his shirt, Stetson, and bandanna, then ducked his face in the spring, cooling his parched skin. He removed his boots and socks, relieving his aching feet by sticking them in the waterhole. He then washed socks and shirt in the creek, attempting to remove some of the dried bloodstains from the shirt. He spread the garments on a rock to dry while he took stock of his situation.

I'm not in too bad a shape, Jim decided. *This cut on my hand doesn't seem infected. I've got a good horse, some food, there's water, and I've got plenty of ammunition. I've also got a canteen and an extra rifle, too.* Besides his own recovered Winchester, there was another in the boot of the stolen bay's saddle. *Mostly I'm tired, and that's nothing a good rest won't cure. I'll sleep until sundown, then head out. Another night's ride, and I should be able to find a place to hole up for a spell.*

Jim checked Cactus' picket rope once again, then settled in the shade of an overhanging rock shelf. He would sleep until twilight, then, with himself and the bay rested, resume his journey deeper into the shelter of the Caprock.

* * *

Another night's travel found Jim far into the labyrinth of multi-hued canyons, cliffs, and breaks which comprise the Caprock. By daybreak, he had located a particularly deep and lengthy arroyo, which he followed to its box end. Jim picked his way up the arroyo's sloping headwall, following a path barely wide enough for the bay to solidly plant his four hooves. Both man and horse were coated with sweat by the time they reached Jim's destination, a wide shelf sheltered by a low ledge of rocks, and scattered boulders which had tumbled from the cliff above. Unusual for this arid region, several springs seeped from cracks in the rock face. Their output gathered in a hollowed-out basin on the shelf, the overflow evaporating before it trickled halfway to the canyon's floor. With water, game to bring down for meat, and sufficient ammunition, a person could hole up here indefinitely, and hold off an army for days. It was an ideal hiding spot for a man on the run.

Jim, however, had no intention of running. He just needed time to prove his innocence, time he didn't have while locked up in a jail cell, waiting to be tried for murder. Jim had hoped to be able to take Marshal Castle along as a hostage when he made his escape, then question Castle once they were safely away from town. Jim was certain Castle would have revealed the truth behind Jenny Cole's murder, if for no other reason than to save his own neck. Unfortunately, the local lawman had made that impossible when he attempted to gun the Ranger down, so Jim had been forced to knife Castle to avoid being killed himself.

Once again, Jim cared for Cactus, ate a few more strips of jerky, washed those down with water from the seep, then settled down to sleep away the daylight hours. Finally confident he had lost any pursuit, at least for the time being, and secure in the knowledge his hiding place could not be approached by any pursuers without his discovering them, Jim would sleep right through the night, awakening with the dawn.

* * *

For almost three days, Smoky McCue had been leading the posse through the Caprock's maze of canyons and draws. Despite the Ranger's assurances they were closing in on Jim Blawcyzk, the others were growing frustrated, convinced that their quarry had long since fled.

"Are you sure you ain't leadin' us on a wild goose chase?" Dude Bannon demanded.

"Yeah, Ranger. Mebbe you're just killin' time and leadin' us in circles while your pardner makes fools of us," Joe Hardy added. "I'm guessin' you want him to get clean away."

"Don't be stupid, Marshal," Smoky retorted. "We're closin' in on Jim. Trackin' through these canyons, over this hard dirt and rocks and checkin' out every ravine and gulch takes time, but we're gainin' on him."

"How can you say that?" Duke Ballantine answered. "We haven't seen any sign of Blawcyzk for miles."

"Duke's right," John Baker agreed.

"I found that spot where Jim camped, didn't I?" Smoky answered. "And we've seen plenty of sign since then. I don't particularly care whether you believe me or not, but I want to bring Jim in as much as any of you, maybe more. It's the only way he has a chance of things being cleared up, and having the charges against him dropped."

"But what if he is guilty?" Baker asked.

"If Jim's guilty, then I want him brought to justice," Smoky replied. "I'm a Ranger, and I'm sworn to uphold the law, no matter how hard that might be, so I won't quit until I track him down."

"All right. We've got no other choice but to go along with you," Ballantine said. "However, if you're protecting your friend, Ranger, we'll make sure you lose your badge… or worse. Landing in prison for aiding and abetting a fugitive's escape would be real hard for you. I'd imagine there are plenty of inmates who'd love the chance to meet you behind bars."

"You don't have to worry on my account," Smoky answered. "Jim came this way."

"I don't see anything," Mike Putney protested.

"You said that horse Jim stole was a bay, right?" Smoky questioned.

"That's right," Putney confirmed.

Smoky leaned from his saddle and plucked a length of black horsehair from a clump of prickly pear.

"This came from a bay's mane or tail," Smoky explained.

"Well, I'll be. You've got sharp eyes, Ranger," Putney admitted. "I never would've spotted that."

"You just have to know what you're lookin' for. That, and years of practice trailin' fugitives," Smoky shrugged. "Let's move. I'd like to catch up with Jim before another night passes."

The posse rode for another mile before Smoky again called a halt.

"Look there." He pointed at a dim trail, which led into a side canyon.

"Once again, I don't see anything," Hardy stated.

"That overturned rock. It's got a scrape on it, a scrape that must've been made by a metal horseshoe," Smoky answered. "Also the dirt's been disturbed, as if the horse wearin' that shoe stumbled. Jim went up this canyon."

"Then let's get after him," Ballantine urged.

"Not so fast," Smoky warned. "Unless you want a bullet in your back, I'd recommend we go in slow and careful."

"That's good advice, Duke," Bannon agreed. "That Ranger could be holed up anywhere, and there's plenty of spots where he could pick us off."

"Which means we'll have to be more cautious from here on in," Smoky replied. He heeled Soot into a walk and turned him into the canyon.

"More sign," he announced a bit later. "See the broken branch on that mesquite? It's pretty fresh. No more'n a day or two old."

"You think Blawcyzk's still in this canyon?" Baker asked.

Smoky shrugged.

"Quien sabe? There's no tellin'. If this canyon's a box, we'll be comin' across him anytime now. If it ain't…"

"Then we've got more trailin' ahead of us," Hardy concluded for him.

"That's right," Smoky answered.

The men wound their way through the canyon for another two miles.

"Up there," Hardy said, pulling his gray to a halt. "Horse droppings."

"They sure are," Smoky said. He reined in Soot and dismounted. Smoky picked up one of the balls of manure, crumbling it between his fingers.

"How old, Ranger?" Hardy asked.

"It's hard to tell for certain, but there's still a bit of moisture left," Smoky answered. "That means Jim came through here not all that long ago. We're gettin' close. Just remember, we want to take him alive if at all possible."

Smoky remounted. He pulled his Winchester from its boot, laid the rifle across the pommel of his saddle, and put his horse into motion once again.

"Let's go, Soot. Slow and easy."

The steeldust snorted, then moved forward at a walk. Scanning every crevice, rock, patch of scrub, or any other possible hiding place, Smoky and the rest of the posse moved deeper into the canyon.

"This arroyo's gettin' narrower. I don't like it," Putney complained. "Are you sure it ain't gonna dead end up ahead, Ranger?"

"I'm hopin' it does, since that'll mean we have Jim cornered," Smoky answered. "Besides, I have a feelin' it'll be openin' up soon."

They rode another mile, until they reached a spot where the trail took a sharp bend to the left. Here the canyon narrowed still more, so that it was barely wide enough for a saddled horse to squeeze between the high, beetling walls. Sunlight failed to penetrate to the floor of the narrows.

"My skin's crawlin'," Putney again complained.

"You can't do anything about that, Mike," Ballantine replied. "There's not enough room to turn the horses around. We have to keep goin'."

"It's gettin' brighter up ahead," Smoky pointed out. "We'll be comin' into the open soon."

A quarter mile further, the canyon opened into a rocky glade. Steep walls, two hundred feet high, surrounded the clearing on all sides.

"Be real careful," Smoky urged as they edged their horses into the opening. They had ridden three-quarters of the distance to the far wall when a bullet slammed into the dirt between Putney's sorrel's front feet, followed by the crack of a rifle shot echoing off the canyon walls. Putney's horse reared, dumping his rider. When Putney scrambled for cover, another bullet threw up dust right in front of him. Putney dove to his belly behind a clump of yucca and pulled his Smith and Wesson from its holster. He cursed his horse as he watched it trot off. His rifle was still in the saddle boot.

The rest of the posse wheeled their horses and raced for shelter. They left their saddles and rolled into whatever cover they could find. Smoky took up a position behind a chest-high boulder.

"You still think I wasn't really lookin' for Jim, Marshal?" he taunted Hardy.

"No. I'd say you found him," Hardy conceded. He stared at the cliffs, trying to ascertain where those shots had come from. "Question now is how're we gonna get him?"

"I dunno." Smoky stuck his head up and a bullet spanged off the rock, just to his left. A second shot, even closer, ricocheted off the boulder with an evil whine.

"Don't come any closer!" Jim Blawcyzk shouted from his position halfway up the headwall. "My next bullet won't miss."

"Jim!" Smoky called back. "This is Smoky! Smoky McCue!"

"Smoke?" Jim echoed.

"Yeah, it's me, your old ridin' pard. Jim, this isn't doin' you any good," Smoky continued. "Come outta there. We'll head back to Quitaque and get this whole mess straightened out."

"I can't do that, Smoke. Those others with you'll plug me the minute I show myself," Jim answered.

"Ranger, you're nothin' but murderin' scum," Ballantine screamed. "We'll get you, one way or another."

"I wouldn't try that, Ballantine," Jim warned. "I could've nailed Putney dead center if I'd wanted. Just get on your horses, ride out, and I won't interfere. But if any of you come nearer, I'll put a bullet in you. Bet a hat on it."

"Ranger, I think I can flank him," Bannon hissed.

"Don't try it," Smoky cautioned. "He's dug in real good up there."

Bannon failed to heed his advice. Bent low, he dashed from behind the mesquite sheltering him and raced for a gully fifty feet away. Jim's rifle cracked, and Bannon went down with a bullet in his chest.

"He got Dude!" Hardy screamed. "That's another killin' you'll have to answer for, Blawcyzk!"

"Don't really matter how many killin's I hang for, does it, Hardy?" Jim shouted in return.

"Jim, listen to me. Give yourself up," Smoky urged, yet again. "I'll guarantee nothin'll happen to you. Otherwise, you know I'm gonna have to come after you. Don't make me kill you, pardner."

"I wouldn't be so certain it'd be you who kills me, Smoke," Jim retorted. "By my figurin', it'd be the other way around."

"He's right, Ranger," Baker said from where he was crouched alongside Smoky. "He's cornered and desperate. You and he might've ridden together for a long time, but that doesn't matter, not anymore. Your partner's turned outlaw, and he's a killer. He'd shoot you down like he'd shoot a rabid dog."

"I can't just give up on Jim," Smoky answered. "Besides, he's forted up real good. If we try to wait him out, it could be days before he gives up, and that probably wouldn't work anyway. Most likely he'd get by us in the dark, or mebbe pick us off, one by one."

"Then what are you gonna do?" Baker asked.

"I'll try and talk to him," Smoky replied.

"You tried that already," Hardy pointed out.

Baker shook his head. "Hardy's right. I doubt it'll work."

"We're about to find out."

Smoky tossed his rifle from behind the boulder, then

emerged himself. He stood in the open, hands held shoulder-high.

"Jim," he called. "Let me come up there, so we can try'n talk this out."

"I don't know," Jim replied. "While we're talkin', Hardy or one of his friends might sneak up on us and put a bullet in my back. Your's too, for that matter."

"I guarantee that won't happen," Smoky promised. "Jim, you know runnin' ain't the answer. We just need to work things out."

"All right," Jim conceded. "You can come up here, alone. I'll be watchin' the others while you do. Any one of 'em even so much as lifts a finger, I'll plug him."

"Hardy! Ballantine! And the rest of you. I'm goin' up there. You heard what I promised Jim. No one makes a move without my sayso," Smoky ordered.

"How long do you expect us to wait?" Hardy asked.

"Give me twenty minutes. By then I'll know what Jim'll do, one way or the other."

"He might shoot you before you reach him," Ballantine noted.

"He might, but he won't," Smoky said. "If he'd wanted to do that, he could have done it already."

"It's your play, Ranger," Ballantine shrugged. "Good luck."

"Jim! I'm comin' now!" Smoky called. He kept his hands held at shoulder height while he made his way across the clearing, then began the climb to Jim's perch.

Dead silence descended when Smoky disappeared from view. The four surviving members of the posse waited tensely, hoping that Jim would surrender, but realizing he probably never would.

The silence was broken by two sudden shots, closely spaced.

"Blawcyzk shot McCue!" Putney yelled. He started to jump from his cover.

"Don't move, Mike!" Hardy warned. "Just wait. If Blawczyk did shoot McCue, he'll plug you as soon as you show yourself."

"Look!" Baker shouted a few moments later.

Jim had appeared from behind the ledge, holding his Colt. He fired three times, then a single return shot echoed across the canyon. Jim clawed at his belly, jackknifed, and toppled over the edge of the slope, rolling to the canyon floor. A trail of dust marked his descent.

Smoky came from behind the rocks, his gun still in his hand. He looked down to where Jim lay, face up in a cluster of cholla. Smoky scrambled down the slope, slipping and sliding until he reached his downed partner. By the time he made the bottom of the slope, the others were already gathered around Jim.

Jim's hands were clutched to his middle, while blood trickled from between his fingers. His face was cut and scraped from his tumble, and his clothes were torn. He looked up at Smoky through eyes glazed with pain.

"You... you plugged me in the... belly, Smoke," he said accusingly. "What'd you... do that... for?"

"You didn't give me any choice, Jim," Smoky answered. "You shot first. I had to drill you."

Smoky's right shirt sleeve was torn, and a bloody gash marked his upper arm.

"Yeah, but... to gut-shoot... your pard..." Jim's voice trailed off.

"I didn't plan things this way," Smoky answered.

Mike Putney pointed his gun at Jim's head.

"Lemme finish him."

"No!" Smoky wrenched the gun from Putney's grasp. "We want to get him back to town alive if we can."

"The Ranger's right," Ballantine agreed. "I'd still rather see him hang... or die slow."

"He can't last. Not with a bullet in his guts," Hardy objected.

"We're still gonna try," Smoky insisted. He knelt alongside Jim.

"Lemme take a look and see how bad it is, Jim." He grasped Jim's arm.

"No!" Jim screamed with pain, clamping his hands more tightly to his belly. "Just leave... me alone, Smoke."

"All right," Smoky answered. "But will you at least let me put a bandanna over that bullet hole, to try'n slow the bleeding?"

"Sure," Jim sighed. Smoky untied the bandanna from his neck and folded it. He lifted Jim's hands, revealing the bullet hole in Jim's bloodied shirt. Smoky used a strip of cloth torn from his shirt tail to tie the makeshift bandage in place. Blood soon seeped through the fabric.

"I hurt... like the... devil. Your slug... sure tore up my...my... guts, Smoke," Jim groaned. Once again, he clamped his hands to his belly.

"How we gonna get him back to town, Ranger?" Baker asked. "He sure can't ride."

"We'll make a litter for him," Smoky answered. "Soot'll pull one. If you wouldn't mind, could the rest of you handle that? I'd like to stay with Jim for a while."

Smoky's eyes were moist, and his voice quavered with emotion.

"Of course we'll do that," Ballantine answered. "I know it wasn't easy, havin' to shoot your friend. That took a lot of nerve. I don't know if I could've done the same if I'd been in your boots. You just stay with Blawcyzk. We'll take care of that litter. You might want to patch up your arm, too."

"Thanks," Smoky replied. "I'll do that. Before I forget, one of you get Jim's gun. It's evidence."

"Sure. Mike, find Blawcyzk's gun," Hardy ordered. "And you'd better load Dude on his horse."

The litter was built and tied to Soot's saddle. Jim, now unconscious, was lifted onto the travois, lashed in place, and covered with a blanket. Dude Bannon's body was draped belly-down over his horse, his hands and feet bound to the stirrups.

"Let's head back," Smoky ordered. His head bowed with sorrow, Smoky put Soot into a slow walk.

* * *

Just before dusk three days later, the posse returned to Quitaque. Curious passersby followed as they rode up to the marshal's office and dismounted.

"You got Blawczyk!" one shouted.

"Yeah, we did," Hardy confirmed. "One of you get the doc."

"Doc Jorgenson's out of town," a man replied. "One of the cowboys at the Rafter 8 took a bad fall from his horse. Doc's out there carin' for him."

"It don't matter anyway," Smoky said, from where he was standing alongside the litter. "Jim's dead. He must've died in the last couple of miles."

Hardy glanced at Jim's ashen face. He put his hand in front of the Ranger's nose, checking for a breath. He felt nothing.

"He's gone, all right," Hardy confirmed. "I'm surprised he made it this far with that slug in his guts. Reckon we might as well take him down to Ike Waters. A couple of you take these horses to Brennan and have him care for them. Have Brennan get word to Duffy McGlynn that we recovered his horse."

"Would you like me to summon the priest for your partner, Ranger?" Baker asked. "I'll have him meet you at Waters' place."

"I'd appreciate that," Smoky sighed. "I guess it's all over."

Jim's body was taken to Waters Hardware and Mortuary. It was wrapped in canvas, then placed in the only coffin available, a plain pine box.

"Don't cover his face, not yet," Smoky requested, when Ike Waters began to wrap the covering around Jim's head.

"All right, Ranger," Waters agreed.

Father Campos arrived shortly after Jim was laid in the casket.

"Ranger McCue. I certainly didn't expect things to end this way," he said. "I'm sorry."

"Neither did I, Padre," Smoky answered. "I'm sure gonna miss Jim. We rode a lot of trails together."

"I understand. Would you like to have Jim's service here?"

"No. Jim always wanted to be brought home to his family if anything happened to him. I'll rent or buy a buckboard from the livery and take him home."

"Of course. However, I would like to bless the body."

"Certainly, Padre." Smoky stood, head bowed and hat in hand, while Father Campos prayed silently over Jim.

"I'm finished," the priest said, as he made the Sign of the Cross. "Ranger McCue, I'm certain Jim asked for the Lord's forgiveness before he died. I believe he will be in Heaven eventually, and I'll pray his stay in Purgatory will be brief."

"I appreciate that, Father. Thank you for everything."

"You're quite welcome," the priest replied.

Once Father Campos had departed, Smoky insisted on covering Jim's face himself, lying his own red silk bandanna over it, rather than wrapping it with canvas.

"Rest easy, pard," Smoky whispered.

He helped Waters nail the cover in place. Several times Smoky, overcome with grief, missed the nails, his hammer splintering the soft wood.

"I don't have another lid to replace this one," Waters warned.

"Don't worry about that. Jim won't care," Smoky replied.

Once the coffin was sealed, Smoky headed to the livery, where he rented a buckboard and team.

"Ranger, I'm sure sorry about your friend," Chauncey Brennan sympathized, "I liked him a lot. I still find it difficult to believe he murdered Jenny Cole."

"Thanks, Chauncey," Smoky answered. "I'm sure Jim'd thank you for takin' such good care of his broncs, if he could."

"Thanks for that, and don't worry about returnin' the

rig. Whenever one of you Rangers is headin' back this way is soon enough."

"All right, Chauncey."

Smoky led the team out of the barn. He tied Soot, Sizzle and Sam to the tailgate. Sam somehow sensed something was wrong, for he allowed Smoky to handle him with no trouble.

Smoky went back to Waters Hardware and Mortuary. John Baker was there, along with Duke Ballantine and the marshal, Joe Hardy.

"I understand you're heading back to Austin," Baker confronted him.

"That's right," Smoky replied. "I want to get shut of this town as fast as possible, so I'm leavin' right now. It's also cooler travelin' at night."

"But what about the situation here? That still hasn't been settled," Baker protested.

"My orders were strictly to find out about Jim Blawcyzk. That's done," Smoky said. "There's too much trouble along the Border right now for me to stay here. Besides, I need to get Jim's body back home. I'm starting out soon as I pick him up."

"But..." Baker again began.

"Don't worry, John," Ballantine broke in. "Our new marshal here will solve all our problems. Isn't that right, Joe?"

"It sure is," Hardy chuckled. "I'll take care of your

complaints, Mister Baker... personally."

"Ranger McCue, you can't leave the town high and dry like this," Baker stated.

"I'm doin' just that," Smoky answered. "I'll tell you what. Once I get back to Headquarters, I'll see if they can spare another man to send up here. That's the best I can do."

"If that's all you can do, I'll have to settle for it," Baker conceded. "But please, do your best to convince Captain Trumbull to assign a man to Quitaque as soon as possible."

"All right," Smoky answered. "Now, if you don't mind, I'd like to get Jim."

Jim's casket was taken from Waters' back room and slid into the buckboard. Sizzle and Sam nosed at the coffin, nickering sorrowfully.

Smoky climbed into the seat, flicked the reins over the team's rumps, and put them into a trot. He left Quitaque without looking back.

Chapter Nine

SEVERAL WEEKS later, Duke Ballantine and Joe Hardy were in the Quicksilver Saloon, taking refuge from the blazing mid-afternoon sun. Both men were nursing beers, while Ballantine idly fiddled with a deck of cards.

"Duke, it's been nearly a month since we got rid of that Ranger. When're we gonna start puttin' pressure on John Baker and his friends again?" Hardy complained.

"Patience, Joe," Ballantine counseled. "It won't be long now. I told you we needed to lay low, until we were certain the Rangers were satisfied Blawcyzk had turned renegade."

"But there hasn't been any sign of another Ranger," Hardy noted.

"I know that," Ballantine answered. "However, another few days won't make any difference. Besides, I hope we've lulled Baker into a false sense of security. With any luck, he won't be ready when we make our next move."

"That makes sense, I reckon," the marshal conceded. He looked up when the batwings swung open. Mike Putney stood there, his face flushed.

"Duke! Joe! You'd better take a look at this!" he said.

"What is it, Mike?" Ballantine questioned.

"Come see for yourself," Putney replied.

"All right." Ballantine and Hardy followed Putney outside.

"Over there." Putney pointed to the empty storefront almost directly across the street from the Quicksilver. A freight wagon and team were pulled up in front of the place. Two men stood alongside the wagon. The first was tall and lean, probably in his late thirties or early forties, with hair graying at the temples. The second was also tall and lanky, but much younger, no more than twenty or twenty five. Slouched on the seat was a third man, whose eyes were covered by patches. He had dark brown hair and a full beard of the same color. A Navajo blanket was draped across his legs. All three men were coated with the dust of long miles.

Two saddle horses, a leggy chestnut and a chunky blue roan, were tied to the back of the outfit. What had caught Putney's attention, however, were the contents of the wagon. It was loaded with kegs of beer, cases of whiskey, and crates of gambling equipment.

"I told you we waited too long to move against Baker, Duke," Hardy hissed. "Looks like word's gotten out that

Quitaque's wide open for business."

"Let's just find out," Ballantine said. "I reckon we should welcome our new neighbors."

The trio crossed the street, and stopped alongside the newcomers' rig.

"Howdy, gents," Ballantine called. "Welcome to Quitaque. Appears like you're getting ready to set up shop."

"Howdy yourself," the older man answered. "We sure are. I'm Jake Hudson. This is my boy, Dave, and the hombre sittin' on the wagon is my brother-in-law, Cord Griggs."

"Duke Ballantine, and the town marshal, Joe Hardy. This redhead is one of my associates, Mike Putney. I own the Quicksilver Saloon, just across the street."

"Pleased to meet you," Hudson said. They shook hands.

Hardy nodded toward the man on the wagon.

"What happened to him?"

"Cord? He's my late wife's brother. They had a ranch outside of Eagle Pass. The place was attacked by a band of Mexican raiders. They killed his wife and two boys, beat and shot Cord, blinded both his eyes, and left him for dead. Somehow he survived, but unfortunately his mind snapped. He can hear some, but doesn't talk, and can hardly walk. My wife, God rest her soul, and I took him in." Hudson lowered his voice. "Truthfully, he's not much good anymore, but on her deathbed Susan begged me to take care of her brother, so I have no choice. You know how it is with kin. I figure he can do some odd jobs around the saloon once we open."

"Actually, since you brought that up, Hudson, what made you come here to start a business?" Ballantine asked.

"I was here awhile back, and liked the looks of the place," Hudson explained. "It seems like an up and coming community, a place where my boy can set down roots. I made some discreet inquiries, found this place was empty and reasonably priced, so I bought it. The High Plains Drinking and Gambling Emporium will be the jewel of the Panhandle. We'll have all manner of games of chance, and the finest beverages. However, no women, at least not yet. We may expand into that later."

"Dad's going to handle the liquor, while I'll be in charge of the gambling," Dave added.

"Hudson, I hate to burst your bubble, but didn't you get word of the trouble businesses have here? Men have been attacked, and property destroyed. That's why I have Mike and several other men to protect my interests. I'm certain they're the only reason my properties have been left unmolested."

"We were assured those problems had been solved," Hudson answered.

"I'm sorry, but you were misled," Ballantine replied. "Isn't that right, Marshal?"

"I'm afraid Duke's telling the truth," Hardy agreed. "There was even a Texas Ranger up here awhile back. He couldn't get to the bottom of things either. Of course, that Ranger turned out to be a bad apple himself. He murdered one of the gals from the Quicksilver, then broke jail and killed the last marshal."

"What happened to him?" Hudson asked. "Is he still on the loose?"

"Nope," Hardy answered. "Austin sent another man up here. He tracked down the renegade Ranger and shot him dead."

"Truthfully, things have been a bit quieter since then, but they can't be expected to stay that way for long," Ballantine added. "Only three days ago, all the windows at Grossman's Dry Goods were busted out."

"We're not worried about trouble, are we, Dad?" Dave said. He tapped the butt of his Colt for emphasis.

"No. My boy's right, Mister Ballantine. I'm positive we can hold our own," Hudson stated.

"All right, let's say you can," Ballantine replied. "There's really not enough business to support another saloon. The customers are pretty well split between my place and John Baker's Panhandle Palace, although I hear Baker's considerin' selling out and moving on. There's a couple other small places, but they don't attract much of a crowd. I'm afraid you'd starve to death within a month."

"I doubt that. We intend to offer high-class entertainment and liquor, much as you'd find in Saint Louis or New Orleans, but at a good deal lower prices. We'll do quite well," Hudson responded.

"Mebbe Duke isn't makin' himself plain enough," Putney growled. "Quitaque doesn't want, or need, any more saloons."

"Are you speakin' for Quitaque, or for your boss?"

Hudson snapped.

"Mike's just offering you some good advice," Ballantine said. "You would be wise to take it."

"You're not threatening us, are you? Because if you are, I expect the marshal here to do his duty and place you under arrest. Or are you also working for Ballantine, Marshal?"

"I'm beholden to no one, but I didn't hear any threat," Hardy stated.

"I'm not making any threats at all," Ballantine added. "However, an intelligent man would realize when he's making a mistake."

"Well, I'm just not all that smart," Hudson retorted. "Plus I've got a stubborn streak as wide as the Mississippi River. We'll be opening the High Plains within a week. Now if you're finished, we have a wagon to unload."

"I'll give you a hand," Putney answered. He lifted a keg of beer from the wagon, then slammed it to the road. It split open, the foaming contents rapidly soaking into the dust.

"Sorry," the redhead smirked.

"Why you..." Dave started for Putney, his fist cocked. His father placed a restraining hand on his arm.

"Easy, Dave. I'm sure that was an accident," Hudson said.

"Of course it was," Ballantine smiled. "I just hope you gentlemen don't have any more 'accidents'. Mike, Marshal, let's leave these folks to their work."

"Nice fellas," Dave sarcastically remarked, once Ballantine and his men were out of earshot.

"Very nice fellas indeed," his father answered. "Well, let's get this wagon unloaded. Cord, let me help you down from there. I'll get a chair and you can sit under the awning, out of the sun, while Dave and I get to work."

* * *

True to his word, Jake Hudson had the High Plains Drinking and Gambling Emporium open within a week. John Baker stopped by at the grand opening to wish Hudson luck, but also warn him to be cautious. If the High Plains was a success, Baker was sure, sooner or later, trouble would arrive.

Duke Ballantine also came by. He took advantage of the free drinks that night, gambled a bit, and spoke briefly with the Hudsons. Unlike their encounter on the street, this meeting was cordial enough. Ballantine lingered until Marshal Hardy showed up. The marshal also had a beer, cautioned Hudson about problems which might arise from drunken customers, warned him to make sure he ran honest games, then left with Ballantine.

Over the next two weeks, business boomed. The High Plains was always crowded, and Hudson had to hire two more bartenders to cope with the crush of customers. Dave ran the games of chance efficiently and squarely. No one could accuse the Hudsons of running crooked games or watering down the drinks.

Cord Griggs spent his evenings at the High Plains sitting near the gambling tables, passing out chips and decks of cards. He merely nodded to anyone who greeted him, occasionally issuing an unintelligible grunt. Quite often, after the saloon had closed, he sat on the boardwalk until dawn, alone, lost in whatever thoughts he had. The sightless Griggs would remain there until some early riser escorted him to the Panhandle Palace, where the Hudsons had taken rooms. Daytimes, he usually spent sunning himself in front of the High Plains. Occasionally, with the assistance of Jake or Dave or a sympathetic townsperson, he would take a short walk to the general store.

While the High Plains prospered, business at the Panhandle Palace, and particularly the Quicksilver, withered. Even Friday and Saturday nights there was plenty of space at the Quicksilver's bar and gambling tables, while even the female entertainers were suffering from the lack of customers. Several of them complained openly about the dearth of business. A few even discussed approaching the Hudsons, to suggest the High Plains might do even better by adding some women to entice more patrons.

"Duke, how long are you gonna sit and let those Hudsons wreck our business?" Joe Hardy grumbled one night. "Even Baker's place is doin' better'n this."

"Joe's right, Duke," Mike Putney agreed. "You've gotta do somethin', and quick. If not, you'll be closin' the doors in less'n a month."

"Yeah. And some of the men you had runnin' scared

ain't so frightened anymore," Tom Frazier added. "You're losin' control, Duke."

"I know, I know," Ballantine testily replied. "I'm workin' on something. Just give me a couple more days."

"That's about all you've got, Duke," Hardy said. "After that, it may be too late to turn things around."

"Don't worry. I'm not givin' up everything I've worked for without a fight," Ballantine answered. "Once I've got my plans set, Hudson will receive a message he won't soon forget."

* * *

Several nights later, Cord Griggs was in his usual spot outside the High Plains. All of the employees had gone home, save for Jake and Dave. They had remained to finish counting the evening's receipts, then lock them in the safe. When that chore was completed, they turned off the last lamp, stepped outside, and closed the doors behind them.

"We're goin' to bed now, Cord," Jake said as he turned the key in the lock. "You comin' with us, or are you gonna stay here awhile?"

Griggs' response was a guttural moan, and he made no effort to move.

"Suit yourself," Jake shrugged. "Well, good night, Cord."

Dave touched Griggs on the shoulder. "Sure wish

you could tell us what you're thinkin'. It'd make me sleep a lot easier. Good night, Uncle Cord. See you later."

Griggs remained in his chair, while his nephew and brother-in-law headed for their room at the Panhandle Palace. They didn't notice the two men skulking in the pitch-black alleyway across the street. Those men watched until the Hudsons entered the hotel.

They waited patiently for another hour, making sure the entire town was asleep.

"He's still just sittin' there, Sid," one whispered. "Reckon it's time to make our move. You think we should cover our faces?"

"Nobody's stirrin', so this is our chance, Race," the other agreed. "There's no need to bother with our bandannas. That hombre's blind, remember? He can't identify us. Let's go." Sticking to the shadows, they crossed the street and approached the unsuspecting Griggs.

One of the stairs to the High Plains creaked when Sid stepped on it. Griggs' head jerked up.

"Hey, blind man," Sid called. "We want to talk to you. You hear me?"

Griggs didn't flinch.

"He can't talk, remember?" Race said. "But he can sure hear. Listen you, we've got a message from our boss for yours. It's real simple, so you can find some way to get it across to him. You tell Hudson he's got a week to close up shop and leave Quitaque for good. If he doesn't, he won't like what happens. You get our drift?"

Griggs nodded, slowly and deliberately.

"Good. Now, to make sure our meaning is plain, we're gonna give you a sample of what will happen if Hudson doesn't take our advice."

Race grabbed Griggs' shirt front and raised a clenched fist, ready to smash it into the blind man's face.

The gun Griggs held beneath the blanket covering his lap roared. Race was driven back into the street by the .45 slug which slammed into his hip. Before his partner, Sid, could react, Griggs turned the gun slightly and fired again. This bullet tore through Sid's stomach, jackknifing him and spinning him around. Sid pitched headlong off the boardwalk. He landed alongside his partner, both men writhing in agony.

Griggs calmly placed his pistol back in his lap.

A light came on in the marshal's office, another in Duke Ballantine's bedroom, over his saloon. Several more flashed on, followed by the sounds of doors slamming and running footsteps as men awakened by the gunfire raced toward its source.

Marshal Hardy was the first to arrive, followed by Duke Ballantine. Several others were close behind. They found Cord Griggs seated quietly, holding his pistol, wisps of smoke still curling from the holes his gun had blasted through the blanket. Race and Sid were lying on their backs, whimpering with pain.

"What happened here?" Hardy demanded of Griggs.

"That man can't talk, Marshal," one of the bystanders

reminded him.

"Yeah. He's not right in the head, either," another stated.

"It looks to me as if these two wanted to rob that poor man," Lila, one of the women from the Quicksilver, said.

"They sure got the surprise of their lives if they did," another spectator remarked.

Ballantine stood over the downed men.

"Is that it? Were you tryin' to rob a cripple?" he demanded.

"Duke, we were just…" Race began.

"You'd better keep quiet, and save whatever you've got to say for the judge," Hardy broke in.

"Yeah. Yeah, I reckon you're right, Marshal," Race said.

Jake and Dave Hudson pushed their way through the crowd, with John Baker at their heels.

"Cord! Are you all right?" Jake asked.

Griggs nodded an assent.

"Thank God! What happened here?"

"It appears these two hombres attempted to rob your brother-in-law, Hudson," Hardy explained. "They never figured on him carryin' a gun. Of course, no one would, bein' as he's blind and all."

"Cord's not completely helpless," Jake retorted. "He

realizes a man with his handicaps can be easy prey for all sorts of vultures, so he carries that gun for protection. He can aim pretty good by sound."

"I'd say more than pretty good," another spectator said. "I'd say dang good."

"Here's Doc Jorgenson," someone said. A man in his mid-forties, carrying a black satchel, worked his way to the wounded men. He knelt beside them for a cursory examination.

"I can't save this one," he noted when he saw the bullet hole in Sid's stomach. Griggs' heavy slug had torn completely through the outlaw and exited from his back. "The best I can do is make him as comfortable as possible."

Jorgenson turned to check Race.

"I might be able to help this man, if I can get the bullet out of him," he said. "However, if he does survive, he'll be crippled for the rest of his life. Some of you get both of them to my office. I'll do what I can."

"All right, Doc," Hardy said. He chose several men to carry the wounded men to Jorgenson's.

"The rest of you, break it up. Go home," he ordered. "There's nothing more to see here."

"C'mon, Cord. Let's go home," Dave said.

"Not quite so fast," Hardy ordered. "I'll need to ask you some questions come morning, Griggs. I know you can't talk, but you can sure shake your head yes or no, or put pen to paper."

"He'll see you whenever you want, Marshal," Jake promised.

"Good, because I'm not convinced this was a robbery attempt," Hardy replied. "I need to do some checkin', and if I find out Griggs shot those men for no reason, I'll arrest him, blind and loco or not."

"I'd expect nothing less," Jake answered. "Just as I'd expect you to arrest those others for robbery and assault if the evidence indicates that, and either should survive."

"I'll enforce the law as I see fit," Hardy retorted.

"Of course," Jake responded. "Now if you're finished."

"I am, for now."

"Good. If you want us, you know where to find us."

Jake and Dave took Cord by the arms, and supported him for the short walk to their hotel. Several times before they got there Griggs' knees buckled, and he nearly went down. Hardy's and Ballantine's gazes followed the Hudsons until they reached the Palace.

Chapter Ten

Sid Starks lingered until the next afternoon, when he died without saying a word. As he'd promised, Marshal Hardy took Cord Griggs in for questioning. Jake and Dave were present during Hardy's interrogation, to help interpret the blind and mute man's answers. Through nods, grunts, and scribbling his responses on a sheet of paper, Griggs managed to convey his version of the previous night's incident, that he had been sitting alone when two men accosted him, threatened both himself and the Hudsons, then attempted to assault him. Fearful for his life, Griggs asserted he shot in self-defense.

"Your story's a bit far-fetched," Hardy said at the conclusion of his questioning. "You claim Starks and Fox said their boss sent them, but didn't name him. You also don't have any idea why this alleged boss would threaten you or the Hudsons."

"It's not so preposterous to believe, when you think of all the trouble there's been here in Quitaque," Dave Hudson responded. "It seems like it might be startin' up again."

"When I want your opinion I'll ask for it," Hardy retorted.

"Dave's opinion is also mine, and also that of a lot of the other business owners in town, Marshal," Jake answered. "Now if you're through questioning Cord, we'll take him back to his room. He's still shaken up after what happened, and needs more rest."

"He'll need more than rest once Race Fox is able to talk with me. If Fox claims Griggs shot him and Starks for no reason, I'll be bringin' him in for murder."

"I wouldn't advise that," Jake cautioned. "It'd be Fox's word against Cord's, and I doubt any jury would take the word of an outlaw over that of a crippled blind man."

"You can't prove Fox is an outlaw," Hardy objected.

"Sure I can. All I need do is check with the county sheriff, or down in Austin if need be. I'd be willin' to bet there's warrants out for Fox... and Starks."

"Mebbe there's some out on the marshal too, Dad," Dave suggested. "We should check."

"You won't find anything on me," Hardy thundered. "Get out of here and take Griggs with you, before I slap all of you in a cell. One more thing: Don't get any ideas about leavin' town."

"We have no plans at all to leave, Marshal," Jake cooly replied. "We have a business to run. Cord, Dave, we're finished here. Let's go."

*   *   *

Business was better than it had been for days at the Quicksilver that night. Sid Starks had been buried within an hour after he died and his partners had repaired to the Quicksilver, where they were drowning their sorrows and toasting their dead compadre.

"We've gotta do somethin' real soon about those Hudsons, Duke," Mike Putney complained. "They're stirrin' up the whole town."

"Yeah," Steve Rawlins agreed. "Goin' after that cripple sure didn't work. You'd better think of something else, Duke, something that won't backfire on us again."

"I've got a couple of ideas," Ballantine answered. He took a long drag on his cigar before continuing. "I've just got to decide which one is best. Don't worry, we'll settle the Hudsons' hash for good. Once we do, Baker and all the others'll fold. This town will be ours again."

The batwings swung inward. Complete silence, except for the scream of one woman, descended on the barroom when Jake and Dave Hudson strode in, their six-guns out and leveled. They stalked straight across the room to where Ballantine and his cronies were gathered.

"What're you hombres doin' in my place?" Ballantine demanded. "Although I have to admit you've got guts, pullin' a stunt like this."

"This'll be a short visit, Ballantine," Jake snarled. "We have no intention of remaining in this snake den any longer than necessary. Don't, or your boss here'll be the first to get a bullet in his belly," he warned Mike Putney, when the red-haired gunman attempted to sneak his pistol from its holster.

Ballantine shook his head at Putney.

"Leave it be, Mike. Hudson'll drill me for certain if you make a move."

Putney shrugged, and let the gun slide back in place.

"Now, as I was startin' to say," Jake continued. "Despite your threats, Ballantine, we were willin' to run our saloon and leave things be, as long as we weren't bothered. We didn't think you'd be so dumb as to try'n run us out of town. The attack on my brother-in-law changed everything, so we're givin' you fair warning. For that, we intend to put you out of business once and for all. Ballantine, if you do have any brains, you'll close up shop and leave town for good. If you don't, we'll come gunnin' for you."

"That also goes for everyone who works for you," Dave added.

Ballantine's face turned red with anger.

"You don't stand a chance against me and my men," he shouted. "I'll grind you into the dirt, Hudson!"

"Take my advice, don't try it," Jake warned. "You'll regret it if you do."

"Get out of here!" Ballantine ordered.

"With pleasure," Jake answered. "Only mark my words, Ballantine. You've got exactly three days."

With their guns still aimed directly at Ballantine and Putney, the Hudsons backed out of the Quicksilver. Joe Hardy stepped onto the boardwalk out front just as they exited. Dave swung his gun to cover the marshal, aiming it at Hardy's stomach. Hardy started for his own gun, changed his mind, swallowed hard, and ducked into the saloon. He'd seen instant death in Dave's eyes.

"What'd those two want, Duke?" he asked, once he was safely inside.

"They came here claimin' they're gonna run me out of business," Ballantine answered. "It's high time I took care of them once and for all. I'll squash them like bugs."

"If you're gonna, you'd better do it fast," the marshal advised. He reached into his shirt pocket and pulled out a thin yellow sheet of paper, which he handed to Ballantine. "Take a look at this. It's a wire Hudson sent this morning. Good thing I asked ol' Jeff Foxx at the telegraph office to show me any outgoin' messages he thought I should know about."

Ballantine quickly scanned the contents of the telegram.

"What's it say, Duke?" Rawlins questioned.

"Hudson's sent to Laredo for some border gunmen," Ballantine replied. "I guess it's time to make our move."

He crumpled the telegram, touched the end of his cigar to it, and watched it flare up. He dropped the paper into an empty glass, staring until it was nothing but ashes.

"By tomorrow night, the Hudsons will be dead," he vowed. "And their place will be a pile of ashes, just like these."

* * *

It was shortly after eleven the next night when Duke Ballantine, Joe Hardy, and a band of ten others burst into the High Plains Drinking and Gambling Emporium. They fired several shots into the ceiling, sending patrons scrambling for cover, ducking under tables or scattering to the sides of the room. Although a few men raced out the doors, others waited in anticipation while Ballantine and his men advanced on the bar, behind which Jake and Dave Hudson waited. Cord Griggs was at his usual spot, seated between the far end of the bar and the gambling tables.

"Mike, you and Daryl get out of the line of fire," Jake ordered his two bartenders. "This isn't your fight."

The two men nodded, then retreated to a back corner.

"You made a big mistake when you opened this place, Hudson," Ballantine growled. "However, threatenin' me was an even bigger one. Now you're gonna pay."

"We'll see," Jake calmly replied. He glanced disdainfully at Hardy.

"I see you're finally comin' out into the open, Marshal."

"I'm just seein' that the law's enforced," Hardy

shrugged. "When you boys open up on Duke and his men, I'll be able to testify they acted in self-defense when they gunned you down."

"So you're admitting you plan to kill us, Ballantine," Jake said.

"And you're in on it with him, Marshal," Dave added.

"That's right," Ballantine confirmed. "We're gonna blast you to ribbons, then we'll burn this place to the ground. Once we're finished here, we'll go after Baker and the rest. This will be my town, Mister. Neither you nor anyone else can stop me."

"I might have something to say about that, Ballantine."

Everyone's heads jerked around to stare at Cord Griggs when he quietly spoke up. The shock of hearing the mute's voice only added to its threatening quality.

"You… you can talk," Ballantine stammered.

"I sure can."

Griggs tossed aside the blanket covering his lap, revealing a heavy Colt Peacemaker in his left hand. He came to his feet and pulled the patches from his eyes. Those eyes glittered an icy blue in the light from the coal oil lamps.

"Blawcyzk!" Ballantine screamed as he recognized those eyes and Jim's voice. "But… it can't be. You're dead! I saw you gunned down. So did Hardy. And everyone here saw your corpse, not to mention the undertaker and that meddlin' priest."

"Don't believe everything you see, Ballantine," Blawcyzk advised, as he pulled his badge from his shirt pocket and pinned it to his vest. "You'd be amazed how much blood you can get from a little cut."

"But there was a bullet hole in your shirt," Ballantine insisted.

"Yeah. In his *shirt*, Duke," Hardy broke in. "He and his pardner played us for fools. We never actually saw a bullet hole in Blawcyzk's belly, just a hole in his shirt and lots of blood. Same thing with McCue's arm."

The marshal turned his attention to Blawcyzk.

"You and McCue took off your shirts, shot holes in them, then put them back on, didn't you?" he said. "Add some blood, and it looked like you'd been in a shootout. Most men wouldn't even question that. Pretty clever stunt, I've got to admit. That's also the reason you acted like you didn't want McCue to try'n patch you up or stop the bleedin'. You didn't want us to notice you hadn't been shot at all."

He hesitated, then continued speaking to Ballantine.

"That's also the reason McCue was in such an all-fired hurry to get Blawcyzk's body into that coffin and out of town. He couldn't chance anyone spotting his pardner alive. As soon as they got far enough from town, McCue opened that coffin, and Blawcyzk popped out of it just like a Jack-in-the-box. Ain't that right, Ranger?"

"That's right, Hardy," Jim said. "Your bought and paid-for lawman's smarter'n you, Ballantine. He figured it out."

"He wasn't all that smart," Ballantine objected. "He didn't figure out your little trick out quick enough."

"By the way, those men behind the bar aren't really named Hudson," Jim revealed. "They're also Texas Rangers, Sergeant Jim Huggins and his son Dan. We're placin' you under arrest for threatening, destruction of property, and conspiracy to commit assault. Once we do some more diggin', I'm certain we'll come up with enough evidence to charge you with the murder of Jenny Cole. Marshal, you're also under arrest. That goes for Mike Putney and the rest of you."

"I'm not goin' to jail," Hardy snarled, with a curse. He started to thumb back the hammer of his six-gun. Before he could fire, Jim shot him twice in the chest. Hardy spun and fell across a table, which splintered under him, dropping him face-down to the sawdust.

The High Plains erupted in a maelstrom of powder smoke and lead. Mike Putney got off one shot, which clipped Jim Huggins' shoulder. Dan, seeing his father hit, returned Putney's fire. The young Ranger's bullet plowed through Putney's belly. The hot-tempered redhead screeched in pain, grabbed his gut, and doubled over. He staggered blindly into a post, then crumpled.

Jim Huggins shot Steve Rawlins through the stomach. Despite the wound, Rawlins managed to lift his gun and get off one wild shot, which shattered the back-bar mirror. Huggins shot Rawlins again, this time in the center of his chest. The slug's impact slammed Rawlins onto his back. He sighed once, shuddered, and lay still.

The gunfight was over in minutes. Seven of

Ballantine's men lay dead or badly wounded, while four others had lesser injuries. However, Ballantine himself came through unscathed. He had burrowed under a card table as soon as the shooting started. Now he emerged, trembling with fear. He stood up and held his hands over his head.

"Don't... don't shoot, Blawcyzk," he pleaded. "I give up."

"All right. Keep your hands up, and stay planted," Jim ordered. "That goes for you others. Toss those guns and get your hands in the air."

The four men still standing in addition to Ballantine complied. The Rangers checked them for hidden weapons, then herded them toward the door.

Jim glanced at Huggins' bloody shoulder. That bullet nick was the only injury any of the lawmen had suffered.

"You okay, Jim?" he asked.

"Sure. It's just a scratch," the sergeant answered. "I'll patch myself up later."

"All right."

"I'm hurtin' real bad, Ranger," one of the outlaws whined. He held his bullet-shattered left arm.

"The doc'll take care of you in jail," Jim replied. He looked at the men lying wounded or dead. "After he cares for these men first. Someone go for him."

"He's probably already on the way," one of the bystanders spoke up. "He must've heard the gunfire."

"That's fine. What's your name, Mister?" Jim asked.

"It's Harvey. Harvey Middleton."

"Middleton, I'm deputizin' you to watch the wounded while we take these men to jail. Once the doc gets here, you accompany them to his office. One of us will meet you there later. You'll also need to choose a few men to get the dead to Ike Waters."

"Sure, Ranger," Middleton agreed.

"Ike's comin' up the street now," another bystander called.

"Good. Middleton, you know what to do. Ballantine, you and your men start for the jail," Jim ordered.

"Certainly, Ranger," Ballantine agreed. The Quicksilver's owner had regained some of his bravado. "I won't be in there for long. You'll have a hard time proving most of those charges, and there's no chance you'll be able to stick Jenny's murder on me."

"I wouldn't bet a hat on that if I were you," Jim retorted. "Now get movin'."

Jim herded the five men still able to walk toward the jail. A crowd attracted by the noise of the gun battle had gathered in front of the High Plains. John Baker pushed his way to the front of the mob.

"Howdy, John," Jim grinned.

"Lieutenant Blawcyzk? But it can't be!" Baker exclaimed.

"It certainly is," Jim confirmed. "Once we get things

settled down, I'll explain everything."

Unnoticed, a slight figure detached itself from the spectators. The figure leveled a gun at Ballantine's back, thumbed back the hammer, and pulled the trigger, firing twice. Both bullets ripped into Ballantine's back, one tearing completely through him and exiting from his stomach. Ballantine, his eyes wide with shock and disbelief, took two stumbling steps, then pitched to his face.

The Rangers whirled, prepared to return fire.

"Don't shoot me, please," Ballantine's killer pleaded, dropping the pistol.

"Penelope?" Jim exclaimed.

The motherly waitress from the Panhandle Palace's dining room had just gunned down Duke Ballantine.

"Yes," Penelope answered, falling to her knees and wailing piteously. "I had to kill him so he wouldn't ruin any more lives. I'm so sorry, Lieutenant Blawcyzk. I'm the one who gave you that poison."

"But why?" Jim asked, shocked at her revelation. Even though he knew he'd been drugged at the Palace, the diminutive, jovial waitress was the last person he would have suspected.

"Duke made me do it," Penelope sobbed. "My husband owed him a lot of money. He lost a fortune gambling at the Quicksilver. Duke promised me if I slipped you that drug he would forget Nils' debt."

"Why didn't you try to warn me, or say something to my pardner Smoky while he was here?" Jim questioned.

"I couldn't," Penelope explained, regaining her composure somewhat. "Duke threatened my daughter. Josie's only fourteen. He warned me that if I told anyone about what he'd made me do, he'd take Josie from me and force her to work as one of the girls at his saloon. I couldn't let that happen, no matter what. Even if it meant you were hanged, Ranger, I couldn't let him do that to Josie!"

Penelope broke down sobbing once again.

"It's all right. Take it easy," Jim advised.

"I know I'm going to jail," Penelope cried, "But I don't care, as long as I know Josie is safe from that monster's clutches."

"I wouldn't say that you'll be going to jail, at least not for long, Penny," Dan Huggins said. "What do you think, Lieutenant?"

"There's extenuating circumstances, that's for certain," Jim replied. "Besides, obviously we can't put Penny in a cell with these hombres."

He looked around for John Baker.

"John," he called.

"Right here, Lieutenant."

"Would your wife mind putting Penny up at your place for a few days, until we can get all this straightened out? She won't be allowed to leave your property."

"May will be pleased to help out," Baker assured him.

"Good. Penny, will you promise not to leave town?"

"I surely will, Lieutenant, and I'm grateful. I don't deserve to be treated so well."

"You weren't a willing participant in any of Ballantine's crimes," Jim explained. "That means a lot."

"I'll take her home now, Jim," Baker said.

"Thanks, John."

"Now, the rest of you get over to the jail," Jim ordered. The last of Ballantine's men were soon locked up.

Ballantine's body was removed to Ike Waters' place, along with the other dead. Two badly wounded men, Mike Putney one of them, were taken to Doctor Jorgenson's. Once they were cared for, the doctor treated the wounded prisoners. Despite Jim Huggins' protests, Jorgenson also insisted on treating the bullet nick across the top of his shoulder. It was an hour before sunrise by the time the doctor finished and departed.

"Now that the excitement's over, it's time to get some shut-eye," Jim Huggins noted. "Mebbe we can even sleep late."

"You and Dan can do that if you want, but I've got other plans," Jim answered.

"What're those?" Dan asked.

"I'm gonna be waitin' in front of the barber shop," Jim replied. "Soon as he opens up, I'm havin' this beard taken off. Mebbe the barber can come up with something to get the dye out of my hair, too. I'm also planning on a nice, long soak in a tubful of hot, soapy water."

Chapter Ten

"I dunno," Jim Huggins answered, rubbing his jaw. "That beard hides most of your face, so I'd say it's an improvement, Lieutenant. What do you think, Dan?"

"Definitely, Dad," Dan answered, laughing. "Anything that covers the Lieutenant's ugly mug sure helps."

"I'm too worn out to even come up with a retort," Jim chuckled. He stretched and yawned. "I reckon you two ranahans are right, we all need sleep. The shave and bath can wait. I'm headin' for bed too."

Once he settled into his room, Jim remained awake long enough to say his evening prayers, despite his exhaustion. He made sure to add his thanks to the Lord for his deliverance from the hangman's noose.

Chapter Eleven

SEVERAL DAYS later, Jim Blawcyzk was back in Austin, along with the Hugginses. They had been reunited with Smoky McCue, and now all four Rangers were in Captain Hank Trumbull's office. Once they were settled with mugs of black coffee, the captain sank into his chair, rolled a quirly, lit it, took a puff, and blew a ring of smoke toward the ceiling.

"All right," Trumbull began. "I've read all of your reports. Duke Ballantine, the hombre you say was behind all the trouble in Quitaque, and the man who attempted to frame you for murder, Jim, is dead. His men are either dead or in jail, and things are quiet up that way. Now, you're gonna explain to me, slowly and carefully, how you pulled off bein' shot dead by your own partner, then comin' back to life, Lieutenant."

Trumbull paused to take another long drag of his cigarette.

"And I do mean slowly," he emphasized. "Unlike what happened the last time you and McCue arrived back here, Jim. Not that I wasn't glad to see you still breathin', after that telegram I got sayin' you were dead. That message hit me like a punch in the gut. It scared me out of my wits. Then you turn up alive, right here in my office. That took another ten years off my life, although I suppose that explains, Corporal McCue, why your message asked me not to tell Jim's wife he was dead, but to wait until you brought his body home, so you and Cindy could help me break the news to Julia. As if that wasn't sufficient, then you two come up with some harebrained scheme to trap Ballantine by openin' another saloon in Quitaque. That's wild enough, but you also want Jim Huggins and Dan to help, and I was just crazy enough to go along with your cockamamie idea. Even tougher, I couldn't let Julia know Jim had come back to town and then headed North again, but had to act as if you had been in the Panhandle all along, Lieutenant. Dunno what got into me lettin' you convince me to agree with your loco plan. By the way, you're all lucky John Baker agreed to buy that equipment and liquor and take over the lease on that saloon. Otherwise, that money'd be comin' outta your paychecks, which would take years."

"Hey, our plan worked, didn't it, Cap'n?" Jim grinned.

"I've gotta admit it did," Trumbull conceded, "But you took an awfully long chance. I still don't understand how you managed to convince an entire town you were dead."

"Well, it wasn't exactly the entire town," Smoky broke in. He took a puff of his quirly, then continued. "Just most of it. And I managed to get Jim's 'body' out of there before anyone caught on."

"Even foolin' the undertaker and a priest. How'd you manage to pull that off?"

Trumbull shook his head.

"Well, first off, I didn't let Ike Waters, he's the undertaker in Quitaque, handle Jim much," Smoky explained. "I just had him help me put Jim in the coffin. I made sure I handled the rest, wrappin' Jim up and coverin' his face."

"But how the devil did you manage to keep anyone from realizing you were still breathin', Jim?" Trumbull wondered.

"You remember Johnny Red Deer, the Tonkawa who used to scout for us?" Jim asked.

"Sure. Why?"

"Indians know a lot of things us white men don't. Johnny taught me how to put myself into a kind of trance. I slow down my breathin', and even my skin turns pale and cooler."

"You mean paler, Lieutenant," Dan laughed.

"All right, paler," the fair-complexioned Blawcyzk conceded. "Anyway, Johnny promised me that trick would come in handy some day. He was sure right. But speakin' of breathin', Smoke, you could have poked a couple more holes in that coffin. It got real stuffy in there."

"I couldn't chance Waters getting suspicious. Besides, I was thinkin' of pluggin' 'em back up," Smoky retorted, laughing. "Guess I missed my chance."

"Who came up with that idea for you to shoot Jim?" Trumbull questioned.

"That was Smoky's idea. I was skeptical at first, but finally went along with it," Jim said.

"He took some quick convincing," Smoky added. "However, when we talked it over, and with the evidence against Jim being pretty solid, it seemed the only way we'd have any chance to trip up Ballantine was if he thought Jim was dead, and the Rangers weren't gonna stay in Quitaque."

"So you shot holes in each other's shirts, but where did you come up with all that blood?"

"Some of it was our own," Jim explained. "Like I told Duke Ballantine, a small cut can bleed a whole lot. You know that, Cap'n. The rest was horse blood. We soaked my shirt real good, so it'd appear I was bleedin' badly. We even filled Smoky's match bottle with some and hid that under the shirt, so I could spill more when needed."

"You actually let McCue take a knife to you?" Trumbull said in disbelief.

"I'm not that loco, Cap'n," Jim chuckled. "Bad enough I let Smoky shoot at me with live bullets and seal me in a coffin. No, I cut my own belly. There's not a chance in the world I'd let Smoky anywhere near my guts with a knife in his hand. Bet a hat on that."

"Cap'n, the most unbelievable part of this whole thing was the lieutenant managin' to keep his mouth shut for days. I never thought I'd see that happen," Jim Huggins said. "And none of his jokes, either. I thought I'd died and passed through the Pearly Gates!"

"I don't talk that much," Jim protested.

"He's delusional again, Cap'n," the sergeant grinned. "Just shut up, Lieutenant," he added, when Jim started to object.

"One more question," Trumbull said. "What about that waitress, Penelope Olsen? The woman who drugged you, Lieutenant?"

"As my report says, she was coerced into that," Jim replied. "Since I'm not pressin' charges against her, the matter's closed."

"All right, hard as it is to believe, y'all managed to pull this off," Trumbull admitted. "However, that still doesn't explain the big hombre hangin' around outside, lookin' like a moonstruck calf."

"Oh, you mean Duffy," Jim answered. "That's Duffy McGlynn. He's your newest recruit, Cap'n. He and I have an agreement. I get Duffy a job as a Ranger, and he won't have me arrested for stealin' his horse."

"What are you talkin' about?" Trumbull demanded.

"When I broke jail, I couldn't get to my horses, so I sorta borrowed Duffy's," Jim explained. "When everything was finally cleared up, I went to see him and apologize. He was still a mite upset, as you could imagine, so we struck a deal. He gets to sign on as a Ranger, and I don't land in jail again."

"You can't do that," Trumbull protested. "What do you know about this hombre? Anything at all?"

"He's a decent enough feller," Jim said.

"The rest of us'll vouch for him too," Smoky added.

"But what about his qualifications? Can he shoot, or hold his own in a fistfight?"

"I dunno," Jim admitted. "However, he's got a real good horse, Cap'n. Nice bay named Cactus. In fact, it was Cactus who donated some of his blood to make my bein' shot look more real."

"A good horse. Figures that's what you'd consider first, Jim," Trumbull sighed. "Well, you might as well tell... McGlynn, was it?"

"That's right. Duffy McGlynn," Jim confirmed.

"Tell him to come in. I'll talk with him, but I'm not makin' any promises."

"I'll get him, Cap'n," Dan said.

A few moments later, Dan returned, accompanied by the big, blonde cowboy. McGlynn stood silently while Trumbull looked him over.

"Duffy McGlynn. I understand you want to be a Texas Ranger," Trumbull grunted.

"That's right, sir," McGlynn softly drawled.

"How old are you, son?"

"I just turned eighteen."

"Can you ride? Shoot? Fight?"

"In which order, sir?"

Bullet for a Ranger

Despite himself, Trumbull had to laugh.

"All right, since all these men here vouch for you, I reckon you're a man to ride the river with. Find a bunk and stow your gear in the barracks. You'll find an empty stall for your cayuse in the stable. Once you get him settled, come back to my office. I'll administer the oath and complete the paperwork to get you formally signed up."

"Yessir, Captain!" McGlynn said, grinning broadly. "I promise I won't let you down."

"Oh, McGlynn, before you head for the barracks, there's two more things."

"What are those, sir?"

"First, stop calling me sir. It's Captain Trumbull, or Cap'n."

"Yessir, I mean, Cap'n," McGlynn answered. "What's the second?"

"As soon as you're officially a member of the Texas Rangers, here is your first assignment. I want you to round up and bring in one James J. Blawcyzk. I understand he stole a fine bay horse, named Cactus, up in the Panhandle. One crime the Rangers can't tolerate is horse stealin'. This here Blawcyzk's a real ugly cuss, and poison mean, so don't take any chances with him. Plug him if you have to. A long stretch in state's prison will do him some good."

"But, Cap'n..." Jim spluttered.

Smoky, Dan, and Jim Huggins were struggling mightily to control their laughter, but failing miserably.

Chapter Eleven

"I'd advise you to make yourself scarce, Lieutenant, before Ranger McGlynn here is able to execute my orders," Trumbull said. "I understand there's a good place for you to hole up, over to San Leanna. If I were you, I'd light out for that hideout right now. Stay there for a couple of weeks."

"You don't have to say that twice, Cap'n."

Jim streaked for the door. A moment later the only trace of the lieutenant was the cloud of dust stirred up by his horses' hooves.

Chapter Twelve

CHARLIE WAS just riding up to the gate of the JB Bar, on his way home from school, when he heard the sound of approaching hoofbeats. He halted Ted, his pet paint gelding, then turned to meet the oncoming rider.

"Dad!" He exclaimed when he spotted Jim. "You're home!"

"I sure am, Charlie," Jim answered as he reined up alongside his son. "It's sure good to be back."

Charlie's collie Pal bounded across the yard to greet them, barking a welcome.

"Pal's looking good, Charlie," Jim noted, "And you look pretty happy yourself."

"That's 'cause I just got a real good report from Miss Abrams," Charlie explained. "She says I'm one of her best students."

"That's certainly fine news," Jim responded. "As I've told you, a Ranger needs to use his brains more'n his fists and guns."

"I know, Dad," Charlie groaned. "If I want to be a Texas Ranger, I have to study hard and pay attention in school."

"That's right."

Jim pulled Charlie's hat from his head and tousled his hair.

Jim's wife Julia had heard their voices, and she stepped onto the porch. Her brunette hair blew in the wind, while her brown eyes sparkled, reflecting her happiness at Jim's return. Jim trotted Sizzle, with Sam in tow, up to the house, dropped his reins, and leapt from the saddle. He took the steps two at a time, swept Julia into his arms, then pressed his lips to hers. They stood there, locked in each other's arms for a lingering embrace. Finally, Julia pushed him away.

"Let me take a good look at you, Jim," she said.

"I haven't changed. Well, mebbe a bit," Jim laughed.

Traces of dye still darkened his blonde hair.

"So I see, but that doesn't matter. You're home, and as usual, just in time for supper," Julia smiled.

Sam impatiently nuzzled Jim in the back.

"I reckon I'd better take care of the horses," Jim said.

"I can do that for you, Dad," Charlie offered.

"There's no need," his mother answered. "Jim, you do that. By the time you're done with them and get cleaned up supper will be ready."

She eyed Jim carefully. "After that, we can talk. Somehow I have a feeling there's a lot you have to say."

"All right," Jim agreed. He and Charlie, with Sizzle, Sam, and Ted following, headed for the barn.

* * *

Later that night, after Jim related all that had transpired in Quitaque, he and Julia were preparing for bed.

"Charlie sure seems happy about school all of a sudden," Jim observed, as he shrugged out of his shirt.

"He is," Julia confirmed. "Of course, I'm not sure whether that's because he really enjoys studying or because he's starting to notice girls. He's been hanging around Jarratt's store quite a bit, and it's not for the candy jars."

"You must mean Mary Jane Jarratt," Jim chuckled.

"Exactly," Julia said.

Jim finished undressing, and was preparing to blow out the lamp and slide under the sheets.

"Jim, please just stand there a minute. I want to look at you," Julia requested.

"Sure, if that's what you'd like," Jim agreed.

Julia gazed at her husband for a few moments, then ran her hands over his chest, down his stomach, and along his ribs.

"You weren't kidding, Jim," she said. "I can't find any new bullet scars. There's no fresh knife marks, either. For once you kept your word, and came home to me in one piece."

"I told you so," Jim softly chuckled.

Julia gently kissed him. As she ran her fingertips slowly up Jim's spine, a thrill ran through his body.

"Don't forget, Smoky shot and killed me outside of Quitaque. You'll be making love to a dead man," Jim warned her, laughing.

"You certainly don't feel dead to me," Julia retorted, "But perhaps this will bring you back to life."

She pressed her lips to his, harder.

"How's that, cowboy?"

"I dunno," Jim answered. "I think you'd better try that again... and again... and again."

Made in the USA
Columbia, SC
23 February 2023